The Acacia Gardens

MARIE-CLAIRE BLAIS

ALSO BY MARIE-CLAIRE BLAIS

FICTION

The Angel of Solitude

Anna's World

David Sterne

Deaf to the City

The Fugitive

A Literary Affair

Mad Shadows

The Manuscripts of Pauline Archange

Nights in the Underground

A Season in the Life of Emmanuel

Tête Blanche

These Festive Nights

The Wolf

Thunder and Light

Augustino and the Choir of Destruction

Rebecca, Born in the Maelstrom

Mai at the Predators' Ball

Nothing For You Here, Young Man

NONFICTION

American Notebooks: A Writer's Journey

The Acacia Gardens

MARIE-CLAIRE BLAIS

Translated by Nigel Spencer

First published as *Au jardins des acacias* in 2015 by Les Éditions du Boréal
First published in English in 2016 by House of Anansi Press Inc.

House of Anansi Press Inc.
www.houseofanansi.com

House of Anansi Press is committed to protecting our natural environment. As part of our efforts, the interior of this book is printed on paper that contains 100% post-consumer recycled fibres, is acid-free, and is processed chlorine-free.

20 19 18 17 16   1 2 3 4 5

Library and Archives Canada Cataloguing in Publication

Blais, Marie-Claire, 1939–
[Aux jardins des acacias. English]
The acacia gardens / Marie-Claire Blais ; translated by Nigel Spencer.

Translation of: Aux jardins des acacias.
Issued in print and electronic formats.
ISBN 978-1-4870-0017-2 (paperback).—ISBN 978-1-4870-0018-9 (html)

I. Spencer, Nigel, 1945–, translator II. Title. III. Title: Aux jardins des acacias. English.

PS8503.L33A9913 2016 C843'.54 C2015-907198-4
C2015-907199-2

Library of Congress Control Number: 2015955233

Cover design: Alysia Shewchuk • Text design: Laura Brady

We acknowledge for their financial support of our publishing program the Canada Council for the Arts, the Ontario Arts Council, and the Government of Canada through the Canada Book Fund. We acknowledge the financial support of the Government of Canada through the National Translation Program for Book Publishing, an initiative of the Roadmap for Canada's Official Languages 2013–2018: Education, Immigration, Communities, *for our translation activities.*

Printed and bound in Canada

To the memory of Mary Meigs

Thanks to Sylvie Sainte-Marie

Thanks to Sushi, a remarkable artist

— M.-C. B.

With much love and thanks for their support and patience to Marie-Claire, as well as my sons, Antoine and Olivier, and Carol Scott-Lanctot.

— N. S.

He went rushing down to the sea, it's really not true what they're saying about me in town, not true, the old john beat me though I never infected him, but they keep saying I did 'cause all us prostitutes and bisexuals gotta be spreading the plague; Petites Cendres was not one of those slick morning joggers, so he had to stop and catch his breath once in a while, leaning against the stone wall along the sidewalk on Atlantic Boulevard, oh he'd forever be running from persecution, as he had been from day one, but where, and above all, how could he escape, especially when Yinn, his personal godhead, had commanded him to go on living and transfixed him with that fierce and fiery gaze like the sun spreading its rays across the very ocean he raced toward . . . yes run, run, Petites Cendres, that headlong dreamer Yinn and his architect had already reached two shining goals: The Rehearsal — a home for young drag queens worn out too fast on the stage — brought to life by the city, by a host of volunteers, in fact the whole community; and another, even wilder scheme, The Acacia Gardens, whitewashed houses nestled in a parkland of mango and lemon trees, better known as "Shipwreck Gardens" to all the men and women left gasping at its edge and every bit as helpless as Petites Cendres was himself, beginning the downward slide so discretely that each snug house was left to enfold its secrets, he, of course, was one of those washed up on the shore before the vast mural of green palms, with "Welcome to Paradise — Welcome All" in great orange letters, and aren't you at least a bit grateful, Robbie said shaking him out of his torpor each day, get up and run, Petites Cendres, your doves and turtle-doves will only take off when you do, so weigh anchor, my friend, I can't imagine what you've got to complain about this time, all that contamination crap is pure, vicious bad-mouthing, so don't pay attention to it, wow, our mural really is something, isn't it, thought Petites Cendres, it won the town's prize for Decor, then think of all the advantages, Robbie said, meals served right here in your room, guaranteed for life, plus access to your Dr. Dieudonné's brand-new clinic with visits every day, what more could you ask for, eh, all this attention and 24-hour care, geez, what else does it take, Petites Cendres, but they're accusing me, and it's all over the papers, thought Petites Cendres, I've got to get out of here, just get away; he was agitated from nights without sleep and this heavy pain in his chest when he ran, bathed in sweat below a mass of hair, and the recurring memory of a drunk, bald man with silver-rimmed glasses, rushing at him, throttling, crushing him up against the wall of the bar, the violence and the weight of his flesh, the fetid breath on Petites

Cendres, he'd promised to be at the man's hotel by eight, and but for that, he'd be at the Porte du Baiser Saloon dancing nightly for customers every bit as repulsive as this one, with heavy-lined eyes behind those glasses, as he cursed Petites Cendres and pushed him to the wall, and in the distant background lay Esmeralda Street and its lean, prowling dogs, who like him, hadn't eaten for days, though his greatest longing right now was for the powder, oh he was hurting for it once more, and the pink wooden houses glowed as he stepped out of the cool shade of the bar into the punishing sunlight, where he'd once been dragged by this man, long before Yinn became boss of the Saloon, the girls outside promoting the evening's cabaret had laughed from high on their heels and beneath their wigs till one of them, Geisha maybe, had said, hey stop beating him okay, you don't want to go killing him on us, do you, good old Geisha, not laughing like the others, that's when the man pushed Petites Cendres away like a dust-rag and said, don't forget, girl, I'll be waiting at the hotel for eight, that's when you get to prove to me what a man, or whatever it is you are, we'll see, I'll make whatever I want of you, that was the moment when Petites Cendres felt more abandoned and alone than ever, but that was before Yinn, his very own Goddess of the Darkened Temples, took over the Porte du Baiser Saloon and became Artistic Director of the cabaret where the girls danced each and every night, at least gentle Geisha'd told the brute, enough already, don't go on tormenting him, stop, but now that same man was accusing Petites Cendres of infecting him, oh such a goddam liar he thought, the client was the one who'd thrust himself on Petites Cendres and terrorized him, but still there'd been no sexual contact, that's how disgusting the old guy was, and here on Esmerelda Street, seeing the ranging dogs and pink houses in the heavy sun, it came back to him that the man had ordered him to bark like the pet he was, then Petites Cendres stood up and leapt on the man out of humiliation for all the beating and abuse, and then gone on to do some beating of his own in the moment of rage when he felt the full mockery of fate, it went back to before Yinn, when Fatalité was still dancing every night, yes, back to before Yinn ever dawned on his miserable existence, yes, back to when Petites Cendres was just one more downtrodden guy, not a man really, more a creature of derision and misfortune, yes, before Yinn or Mabel and her birds, before The Acacia Gardens, before love and hope, and now, here on this day of a calm sea and the wind gently rocking the young palms, their trunks protected by stakes to keep them rooted against the storms and cyclones to come, Petites Cendres had slowed to a walk, then stopped in front of the seaside cemetery and its copper plaques with names now lain to sleep on them, artists, dancers, revered writers who, though they lay in The Cemetery of Roses, were remembered here as well, and Petites Cendres looked away, as though afraid of seeing some he knew, friends and companions, all of them down-and-out, slain by evil and fallen on their plaques like dead soldiers, Petites Cendres was never quite sure, nor did he want to be, as if looking would only confirm the indecency of his being alive while they were not, and who knows if all these young people didn't rise at night to free their spirit-bound energies and talk till dawn, sheltered from the world of day until returning to the chilly folds of their beds under the earth, perhaps, Petites Cendre thought, they do, and what had become of his little Alan who said that, without making love every night, without a man in my arms, what would I be, have you ever wondered, Petites Cendres, oh it's so cold when you, even you, the sexiest of them all, can't be here to warm me, then Petites Cendres began searching for Alan among the plaques shining in the morning sun, and where was sweet Alan, probably left out, a forgotten immigrant of no fixed address, no papers, though he'd lived there so long, sweated away at menial jobs, nowhere to be found now in this phalanx of names which never ceased growing, surely one day soon there'd be no copper left for them all, and where was Alan now, just another wandering stranger on a random road as before, afloat in his freedom, this budding flower seeking only to blossom in sexuality, everywhere and to the fullest, for as Alan used to say, in youth we are inspired by greed and recklessness, and my only fault was to love them all, Petites Cendres thought he heard these words, felt the hand on his shoulder, I could go back home and find myself alone in hospital, still with no one to visit me, what do you say to that Petites Cendres, a less degrading job maybe, guarding rich people's houses during wintertime there, too ashamed of me, no brother or mother to visit me, sure, wash and shine rich folks' homes, would you come see me Petites Cendres, I could get bored real quick you know, and you always know how to make me laugh, always funny with your breast popping out of your blue dress if it's evening, oh that's just to please some coke dealer, Petites Cendres replied, or enchant and entice some guy who's somewhere else was Alan's comeback, 'cause there you are hankering again, then Alan fell silent, disappeared, the last vision imprinted in Petites Cendres' brain was his friend waving from the veranda steps, where he sat bare-chested in white shorts next to a white cat framed by a freshly painted snow-white house, glowing in the heat, its roof ablaze from a shower of jasmin flowers, Petites Cendres asked what he was doing there, and Alan simply said, can't you see, I'm bored, then his body shook with melancholy laughter which was quickly suppressed, it's time for me to think about the future, maybe get a better job, yes, I'm due for it aren't I, but now there was no Alan, no one on the white veranda steps as often as Petites Cendres went by, never a trace of him, no Alain Joseph François in the bars and saunas, nor under any of those pretty names that were the true version, not even on a copper plaque, thought Petites Cendres, nor even in The Cemetery of Roses, where was he then, remembering the nightmares when he managed to get some sleep, long bony fingers gripped him and slid up toward his throat, ah yes it was Her, the cursed, the unwelcome one who had to be shouted at and fought off, its voice promising, I'll punch holes in you, cut you up, for I am the great piercer, yes, I'll cut you up and tear you apart, you with your festering insides, oh sure, the proud, smart Petites Cendres out for a morning jog, but he shot back, I, I'll be the one to finish you, you'll see, but the Hand went on desecrating his innards, while he tried in vain to fend it off with his arms, there's no armour for you my friend, it continued, your arms, your hands are no help to you now, my fingers, though, can seize hold of you and squeeze the pustules till they run in bloody vermillion, thus it was that Petites Cendres suddenly felt the light red blood covering his body, Robbie approached his bed, surely coming to his rescue with the doves and mourning-doves he'd tamed since arriving at the Gardens, but no, of course this couldn't be real, Robbie can't have got here the moment Petites

Cendres begged him to, he had his own life, alone or in Yinn's house, yet the dreams imposed themselves on Petites Cendres with the force of reality, convincing him that Robbie could just fly to his side like his doves, and here was his voice, calming him to sleep, Mabel taught me to fly, it was saying, you need only call me to your side, clawed feet landing like her white parrot on the forged iron rail of the balcony, then motionlessly watching the world and knowing all, maybe it really was like that, maybe Robbie did rush here, high heels and all, to enfold him in his wings. Petites Cendres could understand why Dr. Dieudonné came to visit them once a week, though not the Reverend Stone as well, no one in these gardens which were framed in flowers and giant silvery palms with blade-like leaves, wanted to hear about God, but they did want to remember Fatalité, because he was loved by all, though his ashes had lain under the sea for quite a while now, but according to the Reverend there were souls to be succoured, it's Dieudonné's job to heal your bodies, but mine is to care for your souls recoiling in pain with no hope of strength, the desperate and the insane are all yours, Reverend, Petites Cendres said, and believe me, there are plenty of those here in the Gardens and all around, souls choking on their own secrets, the Reverend said, but exactly who was going to be consoled by the ardour of his faith alone, the Reverend God was just a Father, a magnanimous one, who offered the children his kingdom, and to hear him, thought Petites Cendres, you'd suppose that Fatalité's existence had all been either disorder and surrender or else victories and grandeur, scraping bottom so often as he waded through the debauchery and hours of glory onstage at the Porte du Baiser Saloon, destined solely to be courageous, but surely that was worth something, though this fatherly God made no bargains and kept no accounts, as the Reverend put it, still Fatalité was worth gold, as everyone was, and thus he went his way diagnosing the state of each patient's spirit, taking their pulse, as if preparing to send these angry heads heavenward despite themselves, though they refused to listen to him, amazing, isn't it, he thought, how all these young and not-so-young people could take such care of their sensual pleasures and not their redemption, so out they'd go into the night of excess, still, was this really what drew them to the Saloon and the saunas on quiet, though with an air of secret understanding, to drink and have fun, even when fever told them to stay at home, the Saloon with its antechamber where bodies rubbed each other in lascivious play, as the Old Sophisticate called it when he confided to Petites Cendres, I never go there of course, believe me my friend, when I say they know the end that awaits them and brings them all together even now, I'm too old and experienced to make that kind of gamble, but you, Petites Cendres, you have already lost yourself there my poor friend, really now, don't you regret keeping such bad company, just a little? Petites Cendres, lost in his own brooding, didn't answer, the Old Sophisticate was neat and tidy, different from the other regulars, properly married too, and every evening after he'd had his fill and treated others in a rush of crazy good-naturedness, he went back to the wild animals and brush of his ranch on the archipelago after Robbie whistled him down a taxi, for like other virtuous men he said, he liked nothing better, not the queens available out on the sidewalk, not Robbie, serious and reflective by his side — disguised as what he really was when he didn't work at the cabaret, the Old Man said, a serious Puerto Rican in jeans, sober as a judge and whose gravitas, always a bit funny and provocative around the edges, no longer excited him — at my age said the Old Sophisticate, nothing satisfies me any more, oh hunting and fishing sure, he added rubbing his white beard, Petites Cendres was thinking how Dieudonné spent the whole day beneath the flowery bowers of the cottages, climbing the steps in his white gown to apartments where the frail shadows of men and women fell on mosquito-screens, and even, Dieudonné told him, once in a while a colleague who'd accidentally cut and infected herself, a pearl of blood through a torn glove, nothing really, that's all it took, and as soon as she was well, she would leave to treat families in Africa, he'd come to see her at night, calling her his little saint, unaware of her own sanctity, they'd laugh together, almost crying from joy from their noisy burst of emotion, recalling the municipal ceremony where he'd been honoured by the mayor, but you're the one who deserved a medal dear colleague, Dieudonné said, yes you're the one who operated on them when no one else would, and he'd take her hands in his, telling her she'd soon be ready for her far-off mission, but it had its risks, and how would she be when she returned, her back slightly curved, Dieudonné spent the night circulating through the houses like a giant black swan, so thought Petites Cendres when he appeared at the door and told him to get up and go for a run on the jetty if he couldn't sleep, it's almost dawn Petites Cendres, better get going and breathe the salt air or you'll sink into excess like your friends, really I don't understand you, just loafing here in your damp bed, there's nothing to be afraid of now, so why don't you just get up, or you'll let fear dry up the well-springs of your life, and Petites Cendres said, Dieudonné, don't you know that fear reaches even farther than hope, fear is what's washing us all away here, Dieudonné touched Petites Cendres' roughed cheek with one finger, don't forget your meds, he reminded him before slowly drifting off with the grace of a dark swan, the signs of wear on his face were not lost on Petites Cendres, nor the grey tips in Dieudonné's curly hair, and it saddened him. Petites Cendres knew that if the doctor stretched out these evenings at the Gardens and got home so late his wife and children complained, it was from his attachment to Angel as he withered away beyond comprehension, the student, the schoolboy Angel, expelled from school in another county because the other parents were afraid their children would be contaminated, an abomination, shameful and unbelievable, said Dieudonné, even the littlest children refused to play with him for fear he'd injure himself and spread contagion, he'd complained about this segregation, the crime of expelling a child from school, especially Angel, victim of a medical error, a botched transfusion after a childhood accident, his mother Lina, revolted by such contempt, had implored that he be admitted to The Acacia Gardens, yet still in the safety of his new refuge, Angel became lethargic, weak-willed, and it disturbed his doctor, perhaps it was a reaction to the contempt he'd undergone or simply childish stubbornness that made him avoid lessons with his private tutor, who tried in vain to distract him and rekindle his spirits with electronic tablets and other novelties or surprises, sunk in his wheelchair, he seemed indifferent to everything, Angel you've got to get out of that damn chair and go for a swim in the pool, sure, that's what you need, and if you don't want to study and learn, at least will yourself to try and walk, say, as far as the veranda, you hear me Angel, what are thinking about sitting by the window and staring up at the clouds like that, tell me, at least talk to me or Lina, but Angel said nothing, seemingly absent beneath the placid smile that still concealed his terror, then he got lost in rambling narrations he typed or wanted to dictate to his mother when he could no longer write from continuous coughing or passing out, he had somehow managed to leave his body behind, he wrote, as though looking down from the ceiling at his pitiful body and smile, a pallid creature stretched out on his bed, not yet aware that life had already gone from him, the pale world of men understanding nothing, past or future, this thankless, nasty, worthless world, too pretentious to merit inhabitants, and Angel's misty ramblings that spoke not of God or of angels, but millions of worlds and galaxies as numberless as stars in the sky, interstellar dust he could sail through on the wings of his transfigurations and thrust outward to other universes, his sick body spiralling to them and their darkness, adrift and decaying as it shed ribbons of flesh along the way, and beneath him shone an enternal sun bathing him in its languid warmth, this he wrote, though Dr. Dieudonné had misgivings about this astral paradise, which he deemed unhealthy, and he told Petites Cendres that, unlike him, a child had to be unwanted, dispossessed in the here and now, to fill himself with dreams of eternity like this, surely it was Dieudonné's duty to bring him back to earth and daylight in a fresh dawn of love and tolerance, if it was not too late, he added, for it surely dazzled him, being this far out of body and so close to the blinding sun of Icarus, even as he transcended the misery of his ultimate stupor, a sun in flames, a night of fire to get lost in, and now as Petites Cendres strode slower along Atlantic Boulevard toward the pink and orange glow of dawn over the ocean, he thought on the man who had humiliated him and ruined his reputation, and on the names: Angel, little Alan with no plaque nor sepulchre in the Cemetery of Roses, the herons and pelicans unfolded their wings, and all seemed peaceful on the beach, before the full heat of day, Dieudonné's glance from under the grey tips of his hair, a look of deep intensity that Petites Cendres had no way to define, and which seemed to bear the entire weight of humanity, it made him shudder to think, perhaps because it reminded him of his own mortality, though Dieudonné was not one to lose hope, on the contrary, he was straightforward and under no illusion, victim to no lie, as he told Angel's mother when he said her son could not live long like this unless he ate more and stopped meandering through worlds of delusion, we live in the here-and-now, every one of us, anything else is mad imaginings, why seek out other worlds when we barely know the one we were born to, not even discerned the heart of its mystery, how else could we fail to condemn the futility of hate, not make peace, not listen to the voice of brain and heart urging us to join hands instead of using them for destruction and carnage, and on he ran distractedly, carelessly, hearing Dieudonné's words transfix him from temple to temple, seeing the gaze that reached him and seemed to say, up, up, get up and run for the light before night and dark space close in on you. When I saw you emerge towards us out of the stink beneath our bridges, under the gauzed glare of street lamps, what did you say your name was, Fleur, I thought this one was mine, now here's a confidant and collaborator, this Fleur, this ghost of glory, fallen and buried in the topsoil, Fleur with petals pulled off and crushed, every bit as uprooted as the gypsies I sleep with at night, wrapped in the same covers and scarves, woman and men of no address sleeping out on the ground, pestiferous bodies, spread but still so close to one another they can hear each other's wheezing breath, and when I saw you in your formal jacket, your worn, untidy tux and sweaty, tear-stained silk shirt, I thought, yes, this one's for me, to you alone would I confide my shameful secrets, for you see, my flower-among-ruins, your spirit is pure, thus spoke Wrath as his hand reached out to touch Fleur's shoulder, then as if disgusted with himself, Wrath withdrew the hand, held it suspended, then let it fall heavily onto the filthy, almost crusted coat that wrapped his immense corpulence, remaining upright, almost dignified, he said, you came to us in your torment and your glory, as though the applause following your escape from the concert-hall reached us even here, for the glory you can't bear and the bizarre opera you've written were indeed applauded, imagine you, first an orchestra leader, then all of a sudden, here before my very eyes, and in total disarray, the baton barely out of your hand, the chorus of your dysfunctional music trailing along behind you, unmindful that you were now in a hell unlike any other, listen to me and listen well, young friend, you are mine and you will attend to no one else, a pure spirit has a price you cannot imagine, and I'm not like the rest of them, nor are you Fleur, oh no, they're expecting me for a concert in Switzerland, the young man stammered, for Wrath had breathed sheer terror into him, the gypsies, the travellers, they'll be moving on in their search for mercy, new places to sleep out under the stars, Wrath's contempt was obvious, what are you thinking, my young friend, coffee or wine, whatever's to your liking I'll get it for you, a few more branches on the fire, and others will be joining us for one or the other, the gypsies will come scavenging round the cathedrals and churches and high-end stores until far into the night, with the collars of their damp clothes turned up against the cold, but no one, not one soul will take note of them, that was how I noticed you Fleur, almost heard your music, I thought, this one's mine, not the perfect-but-neglected body, oh no, his soul, yes, believe me, I know bodies, especially children, little girls, I used to be a doctor you see, then a priest, a somebody and no priest is going to jail, no just the low-life rapists, oh they get got alright, in the slammer for good, while I, Wrath, the scourge of God as they said before I was excommunicated, damned man, pariah they called me, and who knows what else, Fleur are you listening, why are you trembling while I'm talking to you, look, there's no one else to hear me in this mire, right, while the morning-after river of suicides from last night or this dawn flows unstaunched, oh they are so many in that current headed straight for their one and only comfort, and why not, hey, I'm talking to you, so lend an ear, I too love music, you know, especially sacred music, listen to me you poisonous flower of a child, listen to how low we've sunk, don't you perceive the beauty of night, all that is near, chants, sacred songs, reaching us from the Cathedral, so Fleur, on a European tour were you, handed to you by that great old musician and composer Franz, once on an evening you told me about the Young Composers' Prize and you in your elegant silk tuxedo, and your mother when she said, you can't do anything for yourself, you need me, I'm coming with you, you can't possibly go without me, but you exclaimed, well I am, all alone, leaving behind even your dog Damien, though you two were inseparable, but you said your friend Kim would hold onto him while you were away, only for a few days, maybe weeks on tour, that's all, and what did Kim say, not a word, nothing at all, she merely wandered off with him to who-knows-where, I sure don't know where, murmured Fleur in the barest whisper, the slightest breath of a small, suffering animal to Wrath's ears, oh yes, thought the old man, like the little girls, the same whisper of a breath as small suffering creatures, not that it prevented me, of course, I sometimes think my senility is that of the human race, he said, all these thoughts slicing through my mind, yet serving no purpose, none at all, till one wonders, did we really commit these acts, true or false, which acts, Fleur asked as he tilted slightly forward in his shoes, still shiny, with the trace of a maternal caress on his feet and his cheek, then the fatal words he'd pronounced, Mama, I'm going alone, and Wrath continued, your friend Clara on posters everywhere in so many European cities, lately, for instance, a Beethoven violin concerto, Elgar's *Enigma Variations*, oh such a profile still somewhat child-like with eyes closed above the bow, I knew young girls with such oriental profiles when I lived in Asia, well, not lived in, more like passed through quickly, safer that way because by then they were on the lookout for men like me, and believe me, it wasn't in any Master Concert halls either, no, in brothels, yes, Fleur said, we were barely twelve, the newest sensation in New York that year, was it Bach or Schubert, twelve, eh, said Wrath dreamily, even when they were seven or eight I couldn't say no, you can't possibly know that forbidden taste, the plucking of such little things as though they were fruit to be nibbled on and eaten alive, it devastates me, besides, you aren't listening to my confession, and if you don't, who will, I wrote a good piece for soprano voice, Fleur said, but hearing it in the hall, I wasn't satisfied, true it was Doctor Death's wife asking, can't this experiment wait a few days till after the little girls of Hiroshima are on their way to school, can't you please, she begged, yes, that was it, a soprano voice for a woman thinking about her own child asleep in the cradle, I thought it was right, but no, it didn't work for me, Fleur said, those gypsies and I, cut in Wrath, we knew how to throw a shelter together and hide our loot in the bushes in daytime, but they keep staging these mop-up operations, tossing out our mattresses and covers, gotta watch out for them, the street-works people don't like us, I've got a train reservation for Geneva, Fleur went on, but they won't be there or anyplace else, everyone's been shipped out, please gimme some change, said an old woman wrapped in a blanket, May's real nice here, her chapped hands tugged at Fleur's sleeve, c'mon kid, dressed up and all, you're taking a tour of where we live, I got a right to ask for something, haven't I, a bit of change is all, I mean you got your musician's salary, don't you, right here in this pocket I betcha, I know I can find something, no, Fleur said, here, lay off me, and gently he closed her hand over something, some bills, who knows what, that's too generous, said Wrath, the old bird's a thief, period, said she had a nice apartment once, then her nephews stole the lot, but can you believe her, we're liars, all of us, take me, for instance, I could be a prince of the Church or who-knows-what, a prince of the garbage-pile, sleeping on a foam mattress with the rats, have you seen that young red-haired gypsy queen standing straight up in her cart over the flaming brazier, the whole camp blazing away behind her as though she and her hair were part of it, and all the while she holds up a crucifix, yelling shame, shame on you for throwing us out in the street — Wrath had whipped himself into exaltation by now — a queen, I say, a poor queen on a horse-cart or a dung-heap, all her belongings burnt, her parents' too, and as he said this, a slight young man approached Fleur and gripped his hand, slanted eyes seeming to mock all he encountered, my name is Su, I'm a drummer, meet Mr. Su, Wrath said, standing like a colossus between them, he dropped a tooth in a street-fight on the way out of some club his group played in, a tooth plus a selection of vowels from his melodious name which he's since forgotten, it was a few months ago in New York, said Su, sometimes his band plays in the Metro, added Wrath, and I've gotta see a dentist, replied Su, hey you wouldn't have a cigarette, would you, Mr. Wrath, the first smoke's a little ritual we share, the latter said as he laughed coarsely, watching Su jam it into the gap in his gum, Su gamely went on smiling as he lit it, too bad, yeah too bad about his career, Wrath went on. Su's a coke-head, that's the club musician's addiction of choice, nothing for him either, so I saw your name in the papers and recognized you, said Su, but this seemed to irritate Fleur as he stepped forward to flee, but Wrath gripped his arm, come on, let's cool off, that was when Fleur noticed Su had disappeared like a puff of smoke, Su never complains, Wrath said, he's my Rising Sun as I call him, very proud, I'll bet he goes back to Tokyo, at least long enough to visit his first wife and his mother and sisters, he's not feeling well, oh he won't say so, but I sense it, he is definitely in the last year of his life, burned from the insides out, said Wrath, my Rising Sun will soon be extinguished, you know sometimes

I went down to the Metro just to hear his group, he has another woman in New York his first wife doesn't know about, Su likes to keep things very close, but all those hidden secrets wind up choking us in the end, don't they Fleur? The doctor's wife, the soprano, sings to him, sleep my child, my darling, then the orchestra comes in, said Fleur as he sniffed the air and caught a whiff of stale smoke from Su nearby, though only his silhouette was to be seen outlined against the river beyond, perhaps after all, Su would never make it to Tokyo nor see any of them ever again, said Wrath, you should have just taken off, you know, Fleur, that audience was way too straight-laced, but they're still music-lovers, and they were there for you, and it happened, Fleur the child prodigy right there on the stage, your own opera, the New Symphony, then the musicians shouting after you at the end, where on earth is he going after such a triumph, and you, wild child, fallen silent like a flashback to the street urchin you were and still are, right as the gates to the kingdom of the rich and famous were opening for you, but you weren't going to any party where the champagne would be flowing that night, were you, no, you got away from them all, I was like that myself for a long while, Fleur, eluding everyone's grasp, especially the judges and magistrates, I bet they're still looking for me, oh think of the appearances and hearings, the low, mean grinding of justice that convicted me for little misdeeds, okay crimes if you must, you know they always keep you around for questioning, in your country they'd have chained me to other inmates who'd served out their time but were still being followed regardless, just to make sure we don't wander into some park where kids are playing, schools, neighbourhoods, all of us chained without chains, no, with a sensor like a heart monitor to report our every movement, day and night, I'm telling you, even the slightest flutter, while I was parked with all those others who'd been freed but weren't free, under bridges and tunnels, oh no human rights league for us, no one, you see we were the unsalvageable, that's how justice labelled us, but Fleur's mind was still on Su, and he asked why, if he was such a good drummer, why he was still down on his luck and living like this, or is he merely passing through like me, I'm telling you again Fleur, said Wrath pompously, your mother and Kim are still expecting you, because after all it's only the beginning of your tour, and you were only gone for a few days, Kim's so quiet it's scary you said, obstinate, ever since the day she found out the Old Salt, champion for both of you, had been killed, and where exactly are those outcasts hiding, nope eh, not a word passes her lips now, said Fleur, to her it was a massacre, when your benefactor died along with the dream of the yellow bicycle, they bludgeoned that to death too, Wrath said, or maybe she clammed up because all you could think about was your concert, not him, not the Old Salt nor of Kim, what if you were the cause of her silence, yes you Fleur, did you ever think of that, take me, I only live for details, said Wrath, it's all in here, the bed of all secrets and their poisonous roots, but Fleur simply said he had his flute with him and if Su wanted, they could play in the Metro together, but only if he wanted to, because Su of the delicate manners and missing tooth that gave the lie to his smile disappeared again, oh he comes and goes, said Wrath, just smokes his first cigarette and takes off to who knows where, too proud to beg though, besides I doubt he's really poor, defenseless maybe, but that's not the same thing, cocaine really did a number on him, Wrath declared as Petites Cendres loped along and recalled the nights out on the town when Robbie rudely shoved him into the car and took him over to the Saloon, come on, he'd say, that's enough loafing in bed at the Gardens, I already have my wig picked out, so all I need is my dress for the evening, Chen gets himself draped in Yinn's transparent dresses cut out in places so you see everything underneath, not so much dresses as paintings really, with little windows you can see their bodies, thin and flowing like dancers in a cloud of confetti, but not me, oh no, he says I gotta lose some weight, and when they dance, the nakedness disappears in motion, you gotta come and see Chen perform in that misty spareness of his and Yinn's latest creations, Robbie said, but Petites Cendres said first he would walk over to the Saloon where Yinn sang and danced or rehearsed his performers, because at this hour the bar would be empty, this time with Robbie he was caught off-guard, not expecting things to have changed so much while he spent his days loafing in his hammock on the balcony with his doves and turtle-doves, waiting for Dieudonné to drop by or phoning Angel on his cell to see if he'd had breakfast, they were all so worried he wasn't eating properly, and Dieudonné had reminded him to call, saying, he has to know we're worried about him, especially with his mother away all day at work, she's alone with no one helping her take care of her sick son the way you have, Petites Cendres had known for a long time that his own benefactor was Yinn himself, first paying for his room and board at Mabel's, then making sure he was looked after at the Gardens, and in comfort too with a bright apartment under the palms, and the mango and orange trees, oh did he feel ashamed at his friend's bounty, was it a sign that Yinn knew the end was near for Petites Cendres, so every step should be taken to make him comfortable, he thought beneath his passion for Yinn, more tender than voracious, underlay this vague sense of shame, though he was afraid every time he entered the bar he'd be stirred by desire again, sure, said Robbie, under those hot dresses there's no mistaking the penis outlined in his white briefs, that's the way it's meant to be, you see everything and devour them when they dance, here, I'll drop you off downstairs, then go up and change, he added on his way up the steps to the cabaret hand-in-hand with the tiny lady holding her little dog in her arms, in his oasis of sloth, his long convalescence, might he have considered it terminal, no, don't let that thought take root, Petites Cendres, no, in his boredom and sobriety, it had never crossed his mind that elsewhere others could be having fun all this time, transforming and renewing themselves each and every day, most of all his friends at the Saloon were never bored with never a thought to what simply went on as before without him, the happiness and pleasure they drew from life, Robbie with new habits, new admirers, and each night climbing the stairs to a cosy nest, or getting into costume with the girls backstage, hearing their laughter, Geisha's cocktails and cherries at the ready, sitting at the bar, Petites Cendres was glad not to have anyone around him as he took in the bar, renovated in these past few months, Yinn loved rotation in his setting, no change was too sudden for him, the seats and stools were re-covered, and on each one the picture of a Saloon celebrity, though Petites Cendres hadn't noticed who he was sitting on, all the faces looked the same as onstage and seemed so intimidating, on the vacant stool to his right was Yinn's face in all its beauty against a background of yellow butterflies,

Fatalité in the act of singing with lips half open and long pendants hanging from his ears, and as if lying on the bench to his left, Herman in his glory days, blue eyes wide and truculent as ever, seeming to say, we decided not to leave after all, so here we are Fatalité and me, right here beside you, what a laugh, Fatalité and his overdose, and me already cold as a stone with Yinn holding me tight and yelling in front of you all, wake up Herman, oh what a gas we had, Fatalité and me, that's all it was, you know, all for a laugh, but hey look, Petites Cendres, here we are back again, and aren't you glad to see us right here on these seats, at that instant a vulgar kid in an unwashed t-shirt covered Herman's face and ordered a drink, then spilled it drunkenly all over the bar and Herman with his blue-green eyes, maybe tonight maybe their hi-jinx would start up again, yes, the painted faces of Fatalité and Yinn still occupied the vacant seats amid the yellow butterflies, like Herman, inviting Petites Cendres to quiet thought, such a difference between them and us, forever inseparable, but where are we, Petites Cendres, Yinn seemed to say, revel in your brief immortality as they did brother, and above all, relax, Petites Cendres, OK, have fun, said Robbie having raced downstairs with the little lady and her dog beside him, rubbing against his gold belt, he was bright and ready for anything in his light and airy dress, 'bout time you got away from those Gardens, hunh, how do you like our new stools, Yinn was right you know, Fatalité and Hermann are here with us, sniffing out our bodies and feeling the echo of drunken customers in their heads, ashes though they are, yep, better this way, for the seeds of life to be cared for once sewn, as Reverend Stone always used to say, good man that he was, God is father to us all, naïve in his beliefs perhaps, he at least tries to bring us peace, as though there was some meaning to Fatalité and Hermann no longer being with us, ha, Herman on his tricycle and arguing with people in the street as he pedalled by, and Fatalité forever singing till all hours, with bristling black lashes, our very own siren of the night, Fatalité, our very own carousel-horse rider, unforgettable in Jason's spotlight, better here than anywhere else, Robbie said, the Saloon with its pews and foyer for communion, he went on like this, waiting for the evening show breathing his word-pictures into Petites Cendres' ear as he memorialized their two dead friends, gone, thought Petites Cendres, gone like Alan, but with no marker like Fatalité and Hermann, he saw the face so clearly that when he leaned toward the painting of Herman's defiant eyes and fleshy lips he secretly whispered, see Alan, you're not forgotten, you're here with us, even if your family left the fragile, weightless fledgeling you'd become to die alone in hospital, rocked gently by a nurse, back in Canada your family showed no concern for you, and an unknown nurse said, it's time to fly my little bird, no feathers or down left on you, yes, it's time, as the old lady approached Wrath, who armed her forcefully away, she turned to try getting some change from Fleur, now there's a boy who's been well brought up, she said to Wrath, not some venerable Monster like you, Mister Wrath, oh you prelates, you'll get yours, same as everyone else, remember I can read palms and I've read yours, she muttered through her scarves, yeah I did it while you were having your nap, I saw all and know all, Mister Wrath, oh yes indeed, everything about you, Wrath spoke to the woman with his usual disdain, back in the day they'd've made a bonfire of your carcass you old witch, too bad they don't any more, but she went on, what's written on you, Mister Wrath, is a furrow of sorrows, and you think you're all alone, but your victims are watching, alone, no indeed I'm not, said Wrath, and as for victims there are legions of us dragging those around till our ball-and-chain becomes theirs and we burden them, why it's the story of life itself, he turned to Fleur, you know, my young friend, I can slip in anywhere like a drunkard's dream before heading for the station, and everywhere I see these multitudes, not one of them knows where he's going or where he's from, guilty of some secret sin though, every single one, that's what they are, smoke-trails of secrets along platforms, yesterday, I spotted one of the regulars, an old slut, the Old Crow I call her, every morning she's there and she's a lot like you, old hag, with your tarot fetish, cartomancy, hooked nose, and black scarf, except she's a clean witch, not filthy like you, still malignant though, she stands up straight and doesn't beg, but she waits saying nothing, I noticed her crow's head and black boots, lugubrious old thing, the Statue of Secrets, maybe she's escaped from some religious order, who knows, she does carry a history of forced submission, and that's always a mark on the slaves of God, a mistake on their part of course that stays with them a long, long time too, while their piety, devotion, and abject nothingness are fully exploited, after all, I am a theologian, Wrath went on, Fleur you're not listening, now what are you dreaming about, oh wait, I know, concert-halls in Brussels or Rotterdam, all those musical cities where they hear the echo of your New Symphony, kind of like Su fantasizing about his intimate jazz clubs in New York, going head-bowed down into the murky Metro or under bridges or to the far ends of railway stations, both of you, yes, I can picture the lot of you, though you don't resemble anyone else, you see that's why I'm confessing to you, as others have to me, oh what a flood of miserable secrets I've heard, if you only knew, whole colonies of sexual criminals in the tunnels underneath monotonous highways, and you know what's in store for them, don't you, ex-cons still imprisoned for life, one day a tornado or flood will entrap them in its rising water, stuck in their holes, hopelessly caught according to plan, that's how they get rid of them, drown 'em all, drastic certainly, but somehow I always seemed to avoid the tentacles of the Law, though I crawled through all kinds of spaces, and one day, or rather one night, on a railway platform, I heard a man's scream rip through the night, maybe some drunkard's lament, but still it ripped me to the very core, you see I can still be attuned to the desperate sound of suffering, for in it was a true despair that froze me to the bone, and I kept on walking, heavy and fat beneath my coat like a shroud, I kept walking with my hat down over my eyes so no one would see, for night or day, stations are always awash in travellers, and that was how I met Su, he asked me for a cigarette and a place to sleep, so I said, follow me, but his slender silhouette disappeared into the fog beneath the arches of the bridge, and he went to sleep with the rats as well, I was getting more and more soaked and frozen through, and it was as though, from that cry, I knew in that instant the full extent of human suffering, theologian and defrocked priest that I was, the unspeakable evil that reigns over us all, be it the cry of a saint or a Hitler, it would never be heard, but only exhaled amid supreme indifference. Bryan was telling Lucia she mustn't forget a thing he was telling her if she didn't want more problems with the police, you mustn't insult them, he said, she'd almost spent the night in jail for that, you don't call a cop an imbecile, so either watch what you say or say nothing, Lucia already had enough problems with her sisters, every bit as bad as my mother the Mayoress who got my black nanny to beat me, they rob you Lucia, right down to your pets, all sent to the Refuge, you don't need any more problems, right, Bryan queried as they sat in his taxi along with Misha whose paws had outgrown the huge basket, a pedal-taxi, that's what he called it when he carried tourists around town, he had taken this job on top of working as a waiter for the breakfast rush at the Café Español, besides they've booked you into the Rest Home, a dying-ground really, Lucia said, it could've killed me, no matter if it was close to the sea, she said, delighted at her escape, they had me tied to a chair, I was too agitated according to them, so I simply up and ran with the chair and all, nobody even noticed, I sure ran fast though, then, as I got close to Atlantic Boulevard, a policeman came over and said, what are doing here with that chair, Miss Lucia, what do you think imbecile, I said, escaping from the hospice, it's not my cup of tea, sure, said Bryan, but don't you see you insulted the man, and you can't do that to the authorities, you have to give way, even if no one really knows why, well anyhow, she went on, I finally managed to get rid of the chair, but if you hadn't come to my rescue, he'd've locked me up for the night, but for you, dear Brilliant whom I love like a son, Lord knows my own son doesn't deserve a mother's respect, nor my sisters, I had to explain to the cop that you were Lucia, and Lucia's innocent, always innocent, no matter what some pain-in-the-neck cop thinks, Brilliant said, and that's exactly what I did, I told him the lady is always innocent, she never even remembers what she's said, and the cop was plain rude: oh so this smart-ass lady is short a few, is that it, is she your mother or something, why'd you stand up for her when she called me an imbecile, you think you can get away with insulting a police officer, young man, so I apologized for you, look Lucia, even if he was rude, I had to be polite, not servile mind you, just a little polite is all, so you didn't spend the night in jail, thus it went as he pedalled them along, he was impressed by the boldness of her escape from the home, chair and all, even pausing to kiss her white hair from time to time, much as he would Misha, who had his own brand of forgetfulness about the long and depressing stay at the vet's, Bryan's memory unfortunately was sharp as a razor, he thought, he'd never forget Misha's rescue from the flood, then his own, from the Second Devastation, no, unlike Lucia, none of it was lost on him, not a scrap, because he kept a written record in his novel when he went home to his room at night or at dawn, after all the pub-crawling, and still recalled the oral version he proclaimed everywhere, parts of it not yet written, as Lucia reminded him, a writer doesn't only declaim, he writes it down, and you never take the time, Brilliant, yes well, I'm busy, he replied, suddenly uneasy, she asked where he was taking them, by now they were on the edge of town, where are you taking me, but she was reassured when he told her that he'd found her an apartment and she wasn't going back to the Rest Home, eternal-rest home that is, nope, he told her, no more having to escape from the dying-ground as you call it, here your sisters can't come and turn you out, no one's going to bother you, I'm taking you to The Acacia Gardens, I've got friends there, Dr. Dieudonné will come see you every day, it'll be good for you to get better nourishment, Bryan said,

I've a feeling your sisters are letting you waste away, especially the way they threaten you, yes, replied Lucia, that's exactly it, they want me to die of exhaustion, they've deprived me of everything, oh how fearsome women can be, but they won't accept me, I'm still healthy, a bit cold and hungry maybe, but at the Gardens they accept everyone who can't get in anywhere else, Bryan cut in, and I'll come and see you every day too, she felt more serene as she listened to him, you're such a good son, she said sadly, thinking also of the treacherous offspring who had abandoned her, never once stood up for or protected her, The Acacia Gardens, yes, I'll be okay there, Lucia said with tears staining her cheeks, cool but pinking in the sun. Fleur was singing, Doctor Death, Doctor Death, low as part of his opera, I wrote that part for a soprano voice, and have you no regrets, Doctor Death, that's in *Extinction*, he told Mister Wrath, without looking at him, as though onstage in a concert-hall, amid the clamour of his music, not even seeing the massive personage in a mud-caked coat who continuously spoke to him in an imposing oratorical voice from a few steps away, that old gypsy woman claims to have the gift of divination, but don't listen to her, Fleur, he said, what I have to confess you will hear from these lips, I was once a fine confessor and spiritual guide, Wrath went on, oh I seized on other people's sins and claimed them for my own, delighted in them, hid in their camouflage like a chameleon, of course a confessor's forbidden to divulge even the worst crimes committed to his care, well young man, I simply used these crimes as my blueprint for the future, as the fervent seminarian faded into the past, nothing more than the vague memory of a submissive child who never considered the risks of his servile obedience to the rules and dogma they bent into him and fed him, nothing I could do, and then listening to men's secrets transformed into the demonic ogre I am now, so what do you think, Fleur, do I not resemble an ogre on the prowl for fresh prey, indeed demonic, you'd say, when all I really do is relieve others of their most abominable secrets, the pediatrician who violates his young patients for instance, was he that person or was I, he'd say, I have a career with a wife and children so no one must know, but you, Wrath, I can tell you everything, and you won't betray me, I'd ask how old they were and for a detailed description of the acts, then I'd finish by asking, aren't you afraid of the law, and he'd say, no, but you alone know all, and I force them to keep it secret from their parents and everyone, oh not by brute force, but they keep it to themselves just the same, after all, I'm a well respected man, you're not listening, are you, young man, yes, well, this man, this pediatrician, like me, has appearances working for him, we highly respectable people, we don't run the risk of exposure in some mediocre trial, no, it's not for us to bow before some vulgar court or other, in fact, the doctor never confessed to rape, only to light touching, nothing brutal, he repeated, after all, it's a branch of medicine where you have to love children and know how to gain their confidence, take the edge off any adverse reaction, so said the doctor, and of course, I listened to him, all the while thinking I am him and he is me, what difference after all between the confessor and the penitent, then suddenly Wrath changed tone as he noticed Su combing his hair, pocket mirror in hand, one can live among ruins and still be dignified, even coquettish, and our oriental friend must be careful before going down the steps to the Metro, or lower still, we are all phantoms headed down to the abundant violence of our haunted underworlds, nighttime especially is right for it, Fleur sang, you'll hear all the little girls in heaven in *Extinction*, the children's choir, Dr. Death, so now don't you regret your words, oh you'll hear them as they're splattered heavenward in firestorms, oh yes indeed, you see, they were all outside on their way to school, you are possessed by this music, aren't you, Wrath replied, vaguely gesturing toward Fleur, who stepped back beneath a stone vault, but what's the point when it all flows from helplessness, if we had the endurance to outwait it with the power of time on our side, things wouldn't be like this, no cruelty, no murder, no, we'd be as we were in the moment of birth, and what is more, we know it, oh we do feel the wound deep within, the hurt of the life that'll be snatched from us, nor do we ever forget it from our first breath to the last, it's impotence that pushes the pediatrician to abuse both his patients and their parents, that is the source of all evil, you'll see, wreaking vengeance for his helplessness on God through His children, they are the instruments of his destructive Rage, this creates a delusion of power, don't you think, Fleur, I didn't tell you that he was one of the faithful who went to church, pious beneath it all, though his faith has been ground to nothing by the destruction he himself wrought, you've stopped listening again, either that or you don't want hear it, anyway I found a bordello in Bangkok and bought myself a boy, who, like you, abhorred me, I'd've done better with another kid called Tai, he was more agreeable, and I found myself switching to and fro, still, I liked the disagreeable one better because of the hate I aroused in him, that impotent, infantile rage, so this, you see, is how demons and ogres such as I approach a child and break him in, Tai was convenient, because he had a servile streak, and the other despised me, said he was ashamed to be seen with me, never wanting us to walk side-by-side, out of haughty embarrassment no doubt, yet possessed of a bitter and supreme beauty, all of which forced me to break him in, and overcoming his resistance was sheer delight, so, rather like the pediatrician, I was suddenly a man of such power, you see, so that the second surprized me more than the first because, although the two sprang from the very same poverty, Tai, the first, was not a beggar, never gave an inch of his integrity, I often bought them directly from the parents in the slums, easy in those days, though today, of course, I'd be hunted down for assault on minors, and even the smallest girls had learned such obscene gestures from men, though they didn't really know what any of it meant, like selling vegetables really, simply doing what they'd learned already, peddling themselves on this ecstatic market of child-flesh, where men of no common sense from anywhere and everywhere, even backgrounds as fine as mine, wandered unaware of the dangers that lay in wait for them, everything a man could desire spread out for sale under the bougainvillia, perfumed spices, sweets to stuff the chosen children and small animals too, oh Fleur, so pure of soul you know no evil, all the more reason to hear what I have to say, but the boy was thinking of his mother and the ticket for Geneva still in the pocket of his evening-wear, the halls where he would hear his opera, indeed he was well-paid and wealthy now, so why was it so important to travel alone and leave her behind, hurt her feelings, telling her on the day he left that she wasn't invited and whatever it was that cut her to the heart, poor woman, so gifted, yet suffering in her helplessness, I feel sorry for you

Fleur, said Wrath, what if for the moment you translate that bottled-up anger into a boiling fervour, I myself am a tepid man and such a frenzy is alien to me, sure things were different once, you are a musical artist, and I was an artist of godly obedience, but what you still don't know is that the flip-side of serving God is the most treacherous of all cruelty, just as the angelic hides the demonic, this you do not yet know, said Wrath, everything, yes everything in this world has its own terrible underside, for we live beneath a hostile heaven of dead or dying stars, detached and disintegrating, I once told you how I loved laughing, and what makes me shake with laughter tonight is Su, ready to go out, his fine hair combed in the pocket-mirror, his hand trembling like a candle in the breeze out over the water, and what veritably kills me with laughter is that this musician seems to feel no disgust whatsoever at being caught up in this garbage-heap of ours, no, none in the least, because all he can think about is the cocaine he'll be getting at dawn, just that and nothing else, such an elegant thought in the darkness of hell, at night, Fleur said, my mother opened her pub overlooking the ocean and refugee families came to dance, even with their youngest children, out on the terrace, and I'd refuse to play for them, rockers and all, there was this selfless priest, Alphonso with her, and they hid Haitians and Cubans in the Church of the Island Archipelago, as I said, Wrath cut in, every man has a hidden underbelly, and your Alphonso is mine, my own antidote, for what he saves, redeems and frees, I scoop up and lay waste, but this Alphonso is an inquisitor to men like me, he wants to do me in, they banished him from a parish in New England for doing too much writing, and here he is hammering away at the sexual abuse of children by priests, and now it's my turn, he's the reason I had to run away, he stripped my vestments from me, all my pomp, and denounced the cardinals of crime, and he dares write attacking the secrets, a whole policy of secrets the Vatican has designed to protect criminals, and I'm still running because he'll find me out again, whatever my new disguise, oh Alphonso knows all about me, when he writes his articles, I know to my stupefaction and horror who he's talking about, yes, he's the very antidote to the hideous evil that is me, this friend of your mother's, Wrath said, he is my judge, and he wants to be my executioner, he and his kind, their sole purpose is to bear down on me with the Wrath of God, the very name I bear, though others carry around still worse secrets and either go to ground or flee to other countries, but a Court on High condemns them eventually — John, for instance, might be a Ukrainian immigrant, now a citizen at last, a successful car manufacturer, living out his life peacefully and bringing up three kids in the exurbs of Cleveland, and who'd ever think he was a danger with a name like that, not a trace of his former self, a fine, upstanding soul with his wife and family of three in their quiet community in the mountains, but in this ruthless world there is a persecutor named Alphonso hunting him down, then up pops the evidence revealing John to be Ivan the Terrible, tangible proof that this senile old man of ninety-one was a Nazi prison guard, barely one step ahead of a death sentence for his vast, clearly documented crimes from yesteryear, yes the most loathsome deeds will out eventually, ah, but John is crafty and, feigning sickness, eventually dies in a German old folks' home, so the old sadist is never put on trial, this most sinister of demonic secrets sleeps to wake no more in the home, ah but

Alphonso the Inquisitor tells us all about the hell that is only beginning for him, Wrath continues, for it is all laid out for John/Ivan le Terrible, but he merely naps on his pile of infamy, leaving his wife and children to renounce him forever, suddenly revealed as he is for the very visage of hell. He never noticed the fleeting shadow of Su combing his hair by the river, similar, thought Fleur, to those last pictures of Jimi Hendrix, cigarette between his lips, looking evasive, like those who have already left the universe behind, off floating elsewhere, yet still minutely attentive to the music he is playing on guitar or drums, always such perfect concentration, this at least remains and rises constantly to the sadness in their faces, fixed till their features seem to fade, a picture to bring one to tears, thought Fleur, well, heaven shines on some of us, like Ky-Mani Marley, but not all of us, not Su, nor Jimi Hendrix, thought Fleur, as Wrath's harangue beat about his ears, and on it went, Wrath was saying, they never tell what follows the beautiful fable of little children come unto the Spiritual Master, of course He can say in all purity, let them come unto me, ah yes, but what then becomes of these little ones, that they don't say, do they, and will their lamb-like innocence be preserved beyond sitting at the feet of Jesus, ah, we know nothing of what befell them, did they turn out to be killers, or would they soil their souls with impure acts, did the Master see beyond their credulity, the naïvety of the small heads turned toward him even as he blessed them, what abject future, what cruelty did they hold in store, these sweet little converts, perhaps they would stone women, crucify men, all as part of the rigidity of their times, surely they couldn't help being cruel, but now, in the exaltation of Jesus' purity, the sweetness of his voice and words, they were convinced that evil did not exist, but would the hand raised to bless them also spare them, or would they die so young being marked for death by the revelation of a love so pure? What if I'd been one of them, what would I have become, would I have known how to value the divine apparition in my own life, or would I have been one of those unfortunates chosen to confront a revelation I couldn't bear, for no ideal of innocence can hold out against the torture of our doubts and the misery of our condition, so Fleur, what do you say, faced with what I'd call our impotence, nothing holds, no, nothing at all, Wrath said, even though, beneath the sun of this May afternoon that would soon turn torrid, he knew the boy wasn't listening, Daniel spoke to the image of his daughter on the computer screen, sweetheart, he said to Mai's somewhat blurry and unstable face, outlined unreliably against a woodland scene on the dark blue screen, Mai seemed surrounded by a campus full of trees as she responded to her father's voice and image, which looked none too stable and direct itself, it must be the wind, Mai said, first smiling, then laughing, this at least Daniel could see as she gave voice to her concern that Augustino might not be at her graduation, you'll see, we'll all be there, including your brother, and I'll do everything possible to be there, Daniel said, your mother and I are so proud of you, though it does date the two us seeing you so grown up, Mai, my little Mai, my youngest, only a few days away from your Art and Photography degree, oh Papa, my life is just beginning you know, you're way too sentimental about us kids, her knowing laugh defeated the silence and her father's hesitation, look, I have to go now Papa, I have a Film class, I have a . . . and so children divide themselves and split away from us toward occupations of their own, Daniel thought, toward elasticity in a universe of knowledge, electrified by fragments borne on a flood of electronic turbulence that belonged to their generation, the computer click closed a door, and the sprinkling of Mai dissolved into the forest of her campus that Daniel pictured to himself, the flat, almost weightless computer under her arm seeming to move in an aura of lightness as part of her, the electronic existence of her age, freed of gravity and skipping dancelike, so it seemed to her leaden father from beneath the weight of his coal-like eyes and greying brows, the same father who let his hair grow long to look younger, but whose gaze, he sensed, had become darker and more suspecious lately, his wife Mélanie, constant herself, was the only one to say he hadn't changed, though of course she made allowances, now to find Augustino in, what was it, India he thought, ah kids forget their father, all they really knew about the boy was that he was writing books, several in fact, while Daniel still laboured over a single one, *Strange Years,* the work of his life, hmm, too bad he'd produced this writer-son, still admired and loved but hard to approach, true he had changed since his grandmother's death, and as the computer clicked off and Mai disappeared into class, he thought back to the bird trapped among the cables in the Madrid station, and even more abominable, the lizard he'd accidentally squashed only this morning, after reading and writing till the veranda was flooded with the light of dawn and, delighting in the smell of tropical dew, he suddenly stood up and stretched toward the sun, a murderous act in the end, as he got up from the lounge chair, a leather-sandalled foot, long and wide, had insolently snared the hind paws and tapering tail of a tiny gecko, small but such a balanced and entire creature, like a man, like himself beneath the thin scales along his green spine, it had been skirting the walls and sliding through the garden grass as though on air, a creature full of curiosity about anything and everything, containing as much beauty as any human face, a more original flying creature than us, its reptilian awareness, thought Daniel, as susceptible to pain and shock as we are, Daniel was instantly conscious of this when out of the luminous, palpitating, red mouth beneath the blue points of its eyes silently blinking in distress, came a cry, not sharp, not even a murmur, but tiny, infinitesimal in the pulsing throat, and yet Daniel could never forget it like the cheeping of a chick searching for its mother among passers-by, or the wing-beat of the sparrow trapped among the cables of a Madrid station, no never forget, the squeaks or moans of so many tiny, innocent creatures we injure or destroy in our habitual day-to-day indifference to anything which is not us, and as the computer shut down on Mai's disappearance with her white sweater, the waves in her short hair, and the brilliant rings in her pierced ears, suddenly, crushing the lizard filled him with anguish, he later remembered the gecko was still moving between his fingers as he laid its small green body in the grass, a protest, however tiny, against this giant and its show of pity, resting among the roses and the yellow hibiscus. Daniel's thoughts turned to Vincent, who had often been hopitalized with his own crises and was studying to be a pneumologist himself, Daniel frequently visited him and continued to be amazed that his son wanted to treat others for his own malady, perhaps it was a desire for triumph over an illness that would be eventually defeated or at least diminished by acts of courage, or possibly it was the relentless quest for happiness that had always characterized him, even when he was little, and in such contrast with Augustino, stubborn in a different way, with an introspection that often turned negative, thinking of Vincent, Daniel thought of those North American cities completely devoted to the comfort, exuberance, distractions, and amusements of student life, boating on the rivers in fall, plus theatres and cinemas specially for them, children of wealth heavily funded by their parents in the studies and comfort that was their due, hence the aura of offhand arrogance shared by the healthy and wealthy in study and lecture halls, day-and-nighttime libraries, while outside in the December and January cold, Daniel was aware of those shut out but still on the fringes of the universities, the poverty-stricken youths lying or leaning along the brick walls, as they panhandled with brownish bottles of wine between their legs, of course he'd seen the snow that fell on their faces and was inhaled between uncared-for teeth, and he felt sorry, wondering how this could happen to them right next door to such elegance and comfort, and he knew, though Vincent was one of the privileged in no danger of lying in the street drunk, cold, helpless, and passed by in oblivion, he would not be like them, this too would be in Daniel's book, he thought, but when he saw his son in hospital and suffering once again, all thought of it had vanished, not to return till today, the cruel nakedness, a little like the lizard, became part of the fabric woven from memories and pitiless images clinging to his memory despite it all, and thus are we contracted, constrained, as though by the revelation of our every gesture, no matter how secretive, amplified by a glass and recalled as sleepy and distracted witness to the least of our daily crimes, Fleur's mother Martha had no knowledge of Haydn or Liszt and told him the Music Council won't be the least bit interested in your opera *New Symphony* or you, a kid who lives in the street, I mean, these are great musicians and orchestra leaders, they'll only put you down as a know-nothing, all that noise you compose, some sort of baroque hysteria, is it even music, the old musician who'd awarded Fleur the Young Composers' Prize came to mind, there was Fleur suddenly cleaned up and well dressed, beaming, and off he'd gone, leaving Kim and Damien the beloved dog who'd shared his cold and hungry nights on the foggy beach, waiting for Bryan to show up with their evening meal and some pot, often covers to keep off the damp too, but in May the nights would be warmer though still humid enough to wake up, their clothes soaked from the mist and eyes empty from hunger, but Fleur was always assured that Damien was well fed, his coat shiny, Kim loved him that much, hmm, how was it his thoughts went back to them again, they seemed to stick to him like their smells, was this why he'd wandered till he met Wrath, even following him under bridges, come have a cup of coffee on me, Wrath had said, where'd you come from anyway, to which Fleur replied, oh close by enough to hear the songs rising in the night sky like a requiem from the cathedral, and he thought of old Franz conducting out on the pavilion platform by the sea after the downtown concert halls were closed by the strike, while in daytime the Roms went to ground and out of sight in the shade of cathedrals and churches, welcome among us young man, said Wrath, here's some coffee I made for you and cookies, though it's a bit cold by now, but you must be hungry, you're all hungry by the time you reach this spot, unlike Kim if she'd accepted Raphaël's invitation to his loft back on the island, he mused, always such a hash smell in that Mexican's studio, oh the drugs flow on, no, not that, thought Fleur taciturn, better the beach or the street, Kim's spirit had closed in on itself as she drifted away from Fleur, Damien too on his leash, you hear me Kim, he yelled, I'll be back in a week, why won't you talk to me, is it my fault, yeah if you can hear me, is it my fault you feel hurt, hell, I loved the Old Salt too, you know, hear that, Wrath cut into his recollection, look my friend, there's always some kind person to bring us coffee or a quart of wine, maybe a sailor or some pious lady, when we pull our mattresses and covers out of the bushes we hid them in during the day, the roads people get on our case, then Fleur felt Wrath turn towards him and grab his silk shirt, practically lifting him off the ground, and smelt the fetid breath all over his cheeks as the hideous face came up against his, listen my friend, Wrath said, maybe you are a talented musician, and some jury has smiled on your *New Symphony*, it's a cantata to destruction, isn't it, this was all supposed to be your re-launch as a child prodigy along with Clara, but you'd better remember you're also a wino whose addiction brought him straight to me, and you're going to have to sleep on the ground with the rest of us tonight, stretch out beside these stinking bodies, if you want to sleep at all, Fleur yelled, leave me alone, no way I'm sleeping with them, I'm not like the rest of you, sure, that's how it starts, but Wrath went on calmer now, weak protestations, like Su when he came to me all so high-and-mighty, yes it's like that at first, but then it passes and you're down in the dirt, the cops burned down the camps the Irish travellers built, threw them right out and torched it all, and that woman standing in front of the flames yelling with her crucifix held on high, oh yes, I can see her, a majestic sign of the end of time, and when they do, they chase us from camp to camp, from country to country, all those holy figures and their burning braziers, Wrath went on, in India one young Tibetan man running in a ball of flames in ultimate rebellion against the Chinese invader, oh and he's far from being the only one, isn't he, the whole world is running on fire with him, their occupation won't get us, no the Chinese won't get us, and ten more monks set themselves alight too under the blue sky and the windy plains, a Tibetan monk in his red robe thinks of all the brothers he'll never see again, walking alone, he can't even bring himself to pray for the crackling of flames in his ears, the young man forever running in flames, no he can't pray as he'd like to, these, these are pictures in the history-book of humanity, said Wrath, from camp to camp, we are chased and hunted, and lo here you are with us now, drink up, have some wine, Fleur, take solace in the fact that you're like that degenerate, syphilitic musician Schubert and the others with your alcohol, but Fleur wasn't listening as his wandering gaze settled on Su smoking cigarettes near the river, over the many bodies that seemed to sleep piled up against the wall, but for the wretched moans that rose from them into the growing dark of night. Angel rolled his wheelchair toward the sun-filled veranda, Dr Dieudonné had told him to make an effort to walk, but Angel thought his legs couldn't hold him any more, perhaps barely enough to get him into the brightly lit bathroom before his mother got back from town this evening, but no more than that, the bus, as blue as the sea, and with fish drawn on the side and lettering that said "Respect the Marvels of Coral", would drop her off at the entrance to The Acacia Gardens, and she'd give a wave of her hand, the brilliance of the bathroom was brighter than anything he'd seen at home, for so long they'd lived in dingy apartments, often in disrepair, moving frequently from one to another so he could go to a different school after being banned, especially since his father was no longer around, he said it was all too hard for him, this repeated banishment, so Angel lived alone with his mother in this brand-new house that would have made him happy if he weren't so sick, so infected and contaminated, that was what they held against him at school, at least here no one reproached him for anything, and on Wednesdays a teacher came to give him drawing and math lessons, he'd never get to use them, he thought as he let himself slide deeper into his chair, so who was he seeing now down in the park, the same ones he usually enjoyed watching, Bryan with his dog Mischa rolling around on the grass, head thrown back and a wolfish grin, plus a white-haired lady who was moving in next door, Bryan said her name was Lucia, and she'll come visit you often like me and bring you presents, but you have to be nice to her and don't sulk, to which Angel replied, but she's a grown-up, how come I'm the only kid here, and lots of them walk with canes and they're almost blind, so how come eh, don't worry, said Bryan, other families will move in, and you'll have friends, besides, I've brought Mischa to play on the lawn, watch him leap around with the turtle-doves and pigeons by the pond, he'd love to go for a swim, why not come with us Angel, but Angel was actually pouting and said he wouldn't come down to the park, he'd simply wait on the veranda in his wheelchair till his mother Lina came back on the blue bus and waved to him as she always did when she got there from work, she'd put the groceries, including desserts for Angel on the kitchen table, though he had less craving for desserts now, and his mother would call him her angel and say he was looking better since he'd started going out on the veranda, Bryan's dog was racing to the pond, and you could hear Mischa bark at the squawking birds, it was often fine out when Bryan came over with Mischa, better than the day before when he'd had all those stomach pains, no, today was different, he hadn't fainted nor seen himself sailing out and above his shrunken body in the wheelchair, hadn't ranged across a galaxy, no, this day was pretty normal, the ordinary kind you live on earth, a day with hopes and expectations, Dr. Dieudonné would be here later, to take his pulse and ask if he had a spot of fever, sometimes there was another doctor with him, she also inquired after his health and said that all it took was one drop to spread through the blood, and it was like that through my surgical glove when I operated, soon I'll be in Africa, she said, but Dieudonné wondered if that was a good idea, I know you truly think it's your duty, but haven't you done enough, taking sufficient risks, and she answered, no, it's never enough, just as Bryan was passing by amid Mischa's barks and the birds' screeching. What if Mabel came for a visit today and brought along her downy white parrot Jerry with the crooked claws, Angel knew those claws would wrap gently around his fingers, and he'd feel the head-plumes against his cheek, as well as the scrape of Jerry's pointed beak on his neck, Mabel would tell him to sing for Angel, now who does Jerry the parrot belong to, she'd ask, the voice as shrill as a flute came back, no, no, Mama, Jerry's waiting for Merlin, where is Merlin, Mama, then Mabel would reach down to her ample bust outlined in red for a handkerchief like when she sang in the Black Ancestral Choir on Sundays and say, I wish you wouldn't go on asking about Merlin, sweetie, really, she'd say wiping away a tear, my Merlin's asleep beneath the red roses, has been for a long time now, oh dear, who killed my bright Brazil bird, whoever it was will get his, no matter what the Lord thinks, sing, handsome Jerry like I taught you, but the scratchy voice would come back, no, no, where's Merlin Mama, at once Angel would feel overwhelmed when Mabel got out her soup and spices and ginger drinks, saying, here, you've got to eat Angel, and don't forget those gingers can raise the dead, but Angel would say, no, no, no, with Jerry repeating every no right after him, no gingers Mama, seeing Mischa shaking himself in the pond, Angel was touched that the dog had emerged triumphant from training school and was no longer intimidated by other dogs, having learned at the vet's to get along with them, and no longer trembling with fear from the Second Great Devastation after he and Bryan had been rescued, water rising above the roofs of houses as the helicopter came for them, you too will get better, Brilliant told Angel, the same as Mischa got over being afraid, hey, his vet even gave him the Best Canine Citizen Award, that got a rare laugh from Angel, Best Canine Citizen, yeah right, what a hoot that dog of yours is, the weather was often fine on days when Bryan came over to the Gardens with Mischa, a citizen like a real person and a comic too, Angel thought, and Bryan said, he may be a dog, but he's people too, he has rights and you gotta respect that. The May sky was pink out over the Atlantic, and such a luxurious atmosphere had been set up for Adrien's interview, answering the journalist's questions seated in a wicker chair on the beach of the Grand Hotel, which served as a backdrop, but still he found it awkward and difficult, and wondered why he'd agreed to talk about his books, I believe you are the most honoured living poet, the journalist ventured, a young man with small glasses in the very latest fashion, as Adrien thought, I bet he's never read my books, but he had all the biographical facts straight, even the embarrassing ones, who knows what his iPad has told him, next, he's going to talk about my widowerhood, how many children I have, whether he was still suffering from the sprain he got playing tennis, and the bad reviews he'd got for his last book, *Faust*, his very daring and personal interpretation of the work, then Adrien heard himself answering brightly, whatever anyone thinks of it, I love writing, and thinking how much of a lie this was given the fact that he frequently detested sitting down at his writing desk at night or in the mornings, his hatred of writing was accompanied by a malicious pleasure that was none of the journalist's business, writing was getting up in the morning during one's feverish youth, thought Adrien, a greedy feeling of joy that few people shared, not everyone being a translator of the classics, nor writing volumes of verse, oh so many books, the most avid reader often being a humble taxi driver when he visited his children in New York, it was the unexpected element in the writing, Adrien thought, you never knew where the seeds would be sewn or where they'd spring up, then he realized he hadn't answered the question, so he covered his tracks and said, you know, sometimes it takes quite a while before you have a body of readers, but that wasn't the case for you and your wife Suzanne, you both became famous quite young, didn't you, the journalist replied as Adrien sniffed the air and glanced at the imposing façade of the Grand Hotel, saying to himself, too bad I'm not on my stone bench next to the tennis courts watching the other players hit the ball to and fro across the net, and why is this stranger talking to me about my wife, what an intrusion, they're all so impolite and ignorant, our first books, both of us, only sold about seven hundred copies, Adrien told him, success, if you want to call it that, came much later on, he felt as though he was indecently displaying their couple to the gaze of a gossipy inquisitor, but still came the questions from the journalist's mouth and the eyes behind those fashionable glasses, this man was going to cut him down, you're over ninety now, said the interviewer, yes, it had to come, thought Adrien, suddenly feeling the heat beneath his white canvas hat, his head burning, at this advanced stage of your life do you sometimes reflect on death, came the question anxiously awaiting his reply, and he said, death is an excellent subject for a poet, perhaps the only one, apart from the changeable weather, look at this sky, it'll be fine tomorrow, so I'll be able to get up early and write, such is my life at present, Adrien replied, in good-natured teasing, did you know this hotel was built a good many years ago, quite legendary in these parts, in fact, and it was designed by my friend Isaac, a titanic architect, well, you know, he's one hundred years old, and he's still building, he is important to the ecology, and it is thanks to him the Florida panther will survive, so you see, not all of us artists live in caves or under ant-hills dream-weaving, Adrien mused on his misleading elegy, wondering out loud, then the interviewer cut him short with a question that could not be skirted, and God, how do you see yourself facing God, once again Adrien rose to the occasion, oh, you have only to read my book on Faust and you'll see, he said confidently, but it's primarily the devil who is discussed in it, came the retort, not God, yes, well several of my friends will be waiting for me on the other side of that invisible door, Adrien went on, I know it'll be just like old times, and they'll all be anxiously awaiting me for happy hour, in fact, they'll already have started without me, I never earned my living from poetry, and for a long time I taught in girls' schools and universities, but my wife, well . . . Adrien cut himself short as though Suzanne were standing right in front of him in the full splendour of her youth, he went on weakly, I was fortunate enough to have a wife who was always youthful and died young, nostalgia and sadness gripped him, and he turned his thoughts to Dorothea, his old Bahamian charwoman, quite a storyteller despite being illiterate, and Adrien had undertaken to teach her reading and writing, it was her he thought of, not Charly who'd be driving him home tonight, here he caused the inquisition to pause, Dorothea had always told him how to dress, and she was the one who fussed over him, you need the white trousers with a white hat today, Sir, she said, and don't get it wrinkled while I'm at church, beware of young ladies dressed as chauffeurs driving you on errands, she said with misgivings about Charly, whom he was seeing too often, oh a man has to enjoy himself, Adrien answered, a man has to have some fun, and I like having her to lunch on our terrace by the sea, yes I do, then he realized he wasn't alone, he heard the song of the waves, yes, he repeated to the journalist, tomorrow will be nice, and I can get up early, the early morning hours are perfect for writing, or else late at night, yes, the night, said Adrien. I have to get back to the hotel by the docks, Fleur told Wrath, it'll soon be night, and I've got to get out of this hell-hole or it'll swallow me, he thought as he removed Wrath's hand from his shoulder, then the older man said, look my friend, no one's stopping you from going back to the hotel, it's only a few steps, I've waylaid you once, but I won't do it again, what's really holding you captive is yourself, not me, in fact it's more like you followed me, oh sure, I led you here, but you were a willing companion, now I know you're disgusted at the idea of sleeping down here with us all, sometimes the women who panhandle in the streets hide the infants here for the night, and during the day they're out with their kids around them, you can see them everywhere in the upscale neighbourhoods where they try for handouts, the kids all swaddled in their filthy diapers are there as part of the come-on, and they say I pervert the youth, when that's the real perversion right there in the heart of that destitute women moulding her child into one more beggar, but can you really blame her, of course not, she's got to feed them, hasn't she, so what choice has she got, eh Fleur, what do you think? There are many mothers and fathers who are forced to sell their children each day, cattle, that's what kids are in this world, let me tell you, it's a pet-market, the wanderers are off and running without ever knowing where they're headed with a boy of eleven holding the bridle of their horse-drawn carts, chased out and their camps flattened, unexpected and unwanted everywhere, another jumbled ghetto is all, then they're off again, leaving only a clothesline strung between two shelters, laundry and kids' clothes still flapping in the wind, sad leavings rinsed once more in the rain, not even able to take along the sofa, chair and bed they wished they could keep, pariahs in the street, whole nations of them, such upheaval that women beg and offer their children to the first comer, when perversion is everywhere, it's really nothing, perversion yes, pity no, Fleur, but you're wrapped up in your music, and we're on entirely different wavelengths, Wrath said, Clara's the special guest at concert-halls, answered the boy, I can still see her face bent to the violin, I will find her, and he felt Wrath's fingers squeezing his shoulder, let go of me, leave me alone, Wrath replied, those women wouldn't be selling their children in the streets, and the thousands of predators like me wouldn't be bickering over their innocence like pulling the shirt off a poor man's back, you see, innocence is out of place in this world, a simple excess of candour that nobody needs, and had we not been born, why we'd still be intact in God's imagination, being born, now there's the real problem, undergoing and absorbing and enduring the blow of existence, for without it we'd never encounter the sadism of our birth into a state of impotent helplessness, never wreak this dictatorship of powerless madness as surely as any king, or despot or straying priest in a far-off palace, and however powerful and bedded in luxury they are, having to push away those who protest and vainly dare to combat them, merely speaking in a vacuum, crowning themselves in the void of their ghost-cities and parading in emptiness, so violent in our despotic and patriarchal guise that the paralysis of helplessness seizes us by the throat, and destroys us, indeed it does, I've seen posters around town, Fleur said, I'm going to hear her play Haydn, you can bet I will, and that will be the last I see and hear of you, Wrath, oh it's harsh to be always so despised, Wrath said, dressed in filthy rags and forever shunned, once feared, once having people kiss my hand, blessings I miss, yes, truly miss, my dear Fleur, once bowed to by multitudes, I can escape justice, but men and women now grab at me all the time, and I can hear the howled insults during my laboured walk toward some station or other, morning and night, and whilst I labour into the wind at dawn by the water's edge, they shout shameful cardinal, degenerate canon, while the rest of my companions sleep, renew embraces or just get up to vomit, I go from stronghold to stronghold with no one, they said if they caught me I'd be in prison for life or maybe something worse, then one day, taking cover under the glare of a station, I suddenly see her before me, the crow-woman, like a statue rigid in secrecy, watching me without speaking, perhaps waiting for a train but never moving, said Wrath, and wishing I could dissolve my thick shadow in the crowd of working-people, going to and fro their outlying zones, those who never really travel, but just, cross through their own stultification in the daytime, awaited in factories or leaving them, heads down and rushing for trains, sweating in their dullness already, imbued and laid low with routine, numbed, bestialized, and without hope, barely noticing the colour of the sky, I wanted to yell at the deafened mob, look at what you're on this earth for, was this subhuman existence really worth being born into, you're never going to be free of it, sometimes I weave through them on the trains, in search of a single face that still has a glimmer of light in this grey mass, anyone who notices me is a vandal, every bit as destructive and ready to do evil as I am, they try to rob the rest, though as bestial as the others, thieving kids ripping off the stunned ones, and they'll insult me right back, you old pedophile, you're marked for death, so get the hell out of here before we do you, that's what they yell at me, so I beat it and go back down to the docks knowing that only the innocent will appease my hunger, yours for instance, Fleur, or Su's, I'm quite confident you'd follow me while pretending not to, both of you, oh you'd walk ahead of me into the secret tunnels by the muddy water, and I'll say that I too love music, maybe you can hear a concert of all sorts of voices nearby, can you hear it now, all sorts of forms and registers, an insidious chorus from hell, oh yes indeed, Fleur, both you and Su enchanted by my sinuous and soft voice telling you both that we're really going to hear Vespers in the Cathedral, or perhaps you'd prefer a Gregorian Mass, once upon a time the Archbishop would conduct the office, whether the choral organ or the Great Organ, the holy chant of the *Kyrie* or the *Sanctus*, come, follow me, we'll sit in the nave and listen silently, and you Fleur, you'll say, oh it's so beautiful, you'll follow me bewitched and unconstrained, Su will too, and in the shadow of a vault I'll offer him his first cigarette, and as we sit side-by-side in the nave listening to the *Kyrie* or the *Sanctus*, it's celestial loftiness will transfigure you, incapable of resisting its hold over you, and I thinking of how the immense Church which has always been my shelter, despite the damning reports of my conduct with children, covering me with its mantle, odorous with many decades of secrets about my abuse, my sacrilege, yes, protected so many times by that self-same Church that I've come to think there's really nothing reprehensible, except perhaps my defiance of God's indifference with acts that proved nothing more than my own powerlessness, and that alone was unworthy, to think of all the archbishops who covered for me so I could achieve the rank suited to my learning and intelligence, none, not one called the police on me, whatever the country, it went through my mind as I warmed up your hand with mine while we were sitting in the nave of the cathedral listening to the *Kyrie* and the *Sanctus*, I told you the choir would be diabolically winning, and through the soloists I heard the voices of children I'd soiled, every single one of them, and by giving me your hand, you alone were able to soften and pacify their cries, Fleur, but then you withdrew your hand suddenly, vehemently, said Wrath, and in the ferocity of your eyes I read how disappointed you were with yourself, and that actually fortified me, reminding me of the high position I had lost, and how many secrets I safeguarded when I achieved that status, I'd protect the most errant priests with my authority, after all we preferred our wealth to virtue, despite our hypocritical sermons, I concentrated on virtue in order to please the women, mothers whose sons I would be taking from them, the intuitive ones sensed that I hated them, that they, all of them, were the core of my problems, they got in the way of my plans, and the vice and ignomy they saw in me were real, for a while, my freedom to do what I liked was unchecked, you couldn't understand the amazing sense of power, Fleur, it's intoxicating, a cold, calculating sort of drunkenness though, derived from the forbidden pleasures of domination over pitiful, defenseless creatures, all victims are pitiful, aren't they now, usually orphans or children sold in the flesh-markets of Asia, not even quality merchandise, other than the tarnished treasure of childhood, what else was there to look for, then suddenly they broadcast everywhere that sexual tourism was outlawed, your mother's friend Alphonso began persecuting and threatening us, doggedly going after us till several were turned over to the authorities, yes, Alphonso didn't work alone of course, we had countless people out after us, and that's when I had to get out, Wrath continued, otherwise they'd definitely take their vengeful persecution out on me, yes, said Fleur, he remembered the choir singing the *Kyrie* and *Sanctus* in the Cathedral, the ticket for Geneva was still in the pocket of his tuxedo, but he'd have to stop at the hotel and spend the night, sleep, ah yes, Wrath went on, many of them never begged till they got here to this den of secrets. Now the interviewer had stopped his oddly intrusive questions, and Adrien found himself in his deckchair alone by the sea, perhaps he'd napped a while and dreamed that some young women had hung a garland of flowers around his neck, led to him by Charlie, though from beneath her cap she eyed him with sarcasm, but as he awoke in the warmth of the sea breeze, Adrien found himself wondering why it wasn't real, why he was alone when his friend Isaac, nearly a hundred years old, was constantly surrounded with youth who warmed to him, the girls even quite risqué at times, was this a blessing or a curse, of course Isaac was legendary for his wealth and generosity, never greedy, but how many of these charming children, beneath their sweet silhouettes as they ate out on the terrace, might dream of relieving Isaac of his fortune, the way Charly had done to Caroline without her even noticing, in fact, consenting more and more to let Charly sign cheques for her, consenting to everything in fact, as she slid down toward the final darkness, although Adrien pardoned Charly, who had simply drawn her employer into certain pernicious games she'd agreed to out of sudden boredom in the absence of her daily companion Jean-Mathieu in Venice, driven to distraction, with all the plans for the future she'd made with him suddenly wrecked, nothing left but nothingness, the poet's death in a foreign land, the man she no longer saw and no longer would see, as Adrien pushed his hat down firmly on his head to keep the wind from taking it, he saw an enchanting couple, wait, wasn't that himself with Suzanne, a couple dressed in white, as they always were when they came to the Grand Hotel for lunch or to see the sun set on the ocean, jolly and full of sweet attention to one another, and unaware of this Adrien watching them in the blinding light of afternoon, such an old-fashioned marriage to be still celebrating so late in their lives, and with such aestheticism and grace of manner, he thought, the woman had taken off her shoes, oh, no, let me carry them for you, the man was saying, and off she went running into the waves, more of a waltz than a rush really, they shared such bursts of daring passion, of carnal sweetness, he thought, they are so like us, as ardent as Suzanne and I ever were, though she did make fun of me for being so stiff, that's what she called me, the rigid intellectual, still I was as tender as this man, melting in tenderness, the slightest contact made me a little more human, how long will they still be together, I wonder, not torn apart, turned out, uprooted, oh but they obviously have no thought of that, ah, how he'd take her in his arms, her white skirts billowing, and sit her on his knee, gazing into his eyes, the man she'd treasured for so many years, in the wooden chair, ah yes, that's it, dance, why not, the slow waltz of two lovers in their twilight years, yet so in love the downward tilt was barely noticeable, as though we too were still together and so united, thought Adrien, true decline was for the dead, not the living who had so much more loving to do, no, then with Adrien's thought, the man suddenly got up and said to his wife, concerned all of a sudden, I'm going up to the room, I'll be right back, and walked enthusiastically toward the hotel, the rivulets ran over in the fountains, and when he still hadn't returned, the woman called him on her cell phone, where was he, had he been taken with something, and why was he in the habit of disappearing so often like this, but she couldn't reach him, or perhaps, thought Adrien, as he saw the uneasiness in her eyes blinking from the sun, the phone is malfunctioning, God, where was he, ah, there he was beside her again, she with her arms outstretched in complete assurance, so like Suzanne and Adrien they were, a bouquet of flowers, birds of paradise, was placed in the woman's arms, my love, he said, my love, then a rock group struck up from the other side of bar and drew Adrien's attention away from them, we love rock'n'roll sang the young kids, but the ecstatic couple seemed neither to hear nor see them, Adrien's left ear had been annoying him lately by amplifying the sounds it encountered, and he heard louder than life the words he did not want to hear, we love rock'n'roll, maybe the couple was deaf or only heard the slapping of the waves and what they said to one another, what nasty tricks old age plays, he thought, hearing what I don't want to, we love rock and roll, we love rock and roll, now was the time to get out his notebook and write something, while it engraved itself on his eardrums, he saw his tanned hand, come to rest on the white sheet and, though brown and wrinkled, it was the fine hand of a writer, he thought with some pride, long and supple fingers, he bent over the poem he'd ceaselessly reworked, touched up, twisted, and cut, he was still on "Giving Account", he wearied of rereading it, anyway giving account to whom, about what, and why giving account, his eyes wandered back to the enchanted couple as full of sunshine as the day, and the dogged interviewer's question kept coming back, dear poet, what will you say to God when you meet Him, or rather the opposite, what will He say to you, wondered Adrien, perhaps that there are too many poets in paradise, not all of his exceptional calibre of course, and Adrien would reply, I dearly wish to see my wife so we can begin our life together again, and on that hope, Adrien felt himself in the grip of a gentle sleepiness, though he was in no hurry to meet God, as the interviewer put it, even if it made no sense, first he had to finish his book on Marlowe's *Faust*, three or four translations from English, and the poem, well, "Giving Account" would never be finished, would it, he really thought about it, no, that way lies the path of regrets, then maybe he'd change the title, of course, that's it, he thought, he'd refocus on the ecstasy of the old Suzanne-and-Adrien couple in the sunlight instead, yes, he dozed shaded by his hat, muttering that life was such a magnificent gift, lavishing revelations, even miracles, on him every single day till he was spoiled, what more could one wish for, except perhaps supper on the terrace with Charly, then a spin in the black limo on race day, dream, dream, he thought, as poets and madmen dream, painters as well dream, of some irreparable fling that an old man such as himself, charming and elegant as he still was, had no right to, so perhaps in the end, the sin for which he had to give account was simply that of being a concupiscent dreamer, but was that really so bad, he wondered with a smile of satisfaction. Su's cough was deep and hollow-sounding, as he combed his fine hair looking in the pocket-mirror, perhaps he'd never see Tokyo or his mother and wife again, Wrath opined, they might still take him in at a hospital or dispensary, they do that, scoop up the wretched with a shovel, then shove them into an ambulance for the night, never to be seen again, it's too late by the sound of that awful cough, Fleur, he'll be sleeping on the ground tonight with the bitter smell of other people's wine all around him, or maybe play music in the Metro, and to finish he'll sing *La Vie en Rose* for a baggie of cocaine reminding himself of a woman he once loved, he'll always have that gap in his teeth with a cigarette stuck in it, forging on with no lack of courage, you'll hear him singing *La Vie en Rose* for us into the night, then hearing Su cough again, Fleur cried, he's really not well, he mustn't die here, no way, I'll take him to my hotel so he can sleep in the warm, yeah, and I'll call an ambulance, oh really, how noble of you, Wrath cut in, I'm telling you, Fleur, it's too late, that was when the boy envisioned Kim with the dogs Damien and Max leashed by her side and on their way to the beach, Jérôme the African was with them too, as though in a coma, dragging his bike overloaded with water bottles and rags, they all looked starved and had obviously been sleeping out in the cold and damp of spring, it was Su's cough that reminded him of all the other nights on the beaches like theirs, as well as Kim's obtuse expression, quiet as ever, never willing to talk about the Old Salt's murder at the hands of two thugs they never found, it was as though Su's cough opened a groove in Fleur's spirit, inflamed and swollen, and Jérôme the African's words did that too, sung plaintively while he beat on Kim's tambourine: pillage I've seen in the streets of the Ivory Coast, pillage and rape, when I was a boy-soldier, so many, oh so many, long live the unpunished, the recruiters of kids, oh so much raping and pillaging, he sang, in a jumble of words as though he'd forgotten what the words actually meant, and often a crown of greenery on his head, cactus flowers with sharp thorns, or woven grass of some kind that wafted in the breeze as he walked indeterminately, as though floating like the misfortune that hovered over him as he walked, the faint, impalpable sadness of the child-soldier crowned with flowers and thorns, not the Jérôme who peddled drugs like so many others, thought Fleur as the engorged channel of memory opened wide to all of them, Jérôme, Kim, Damien, Max, to the long wait on beaches and docks at night, sometimes walking the whole night through, wary of police surveillance until dawn, now Fleur felt the grossness of Wrath by his side and heard that voice again, not gross at all, but rather firm and imposing, almost theatrical at times, as though echoing the sound of the water, the slapping of wavelets on the river nearby, I'm telling you, Fleur, the wandering tribes of pariahs won't always sleep as soundly as they do tonight on the ground amid garbage, they've got to drop somewhere, worn out, beaten from pillar to post in despair wherever they go, suddenly defeated and literally tumbling, grazing the stone or concrete walls with their shadows as they do, with no more sound than pebbles tossed by a distracted hand, yet these are living beings, women and children, and guess what they'll be doing tomorrow, no longer able to bear the waiting, the contempt, and their subhuman existence, they'll force open windows in houses where the rich, sit behind the blinds and shutters at heavy-laden tables and take their leftovers with a yelp, after killing the hosts of course, still yapping like starving foxes as they cut throats, no guns needed, just the skilled hands of instinctive killers, believe me, Fleur, their joy has been in planning this orgy of carnage for a long time, then going from one house to the next, storefronts will be the next to go, hundreds, thousands of them, oh I can see them now, Wrath said, we've never witnessed the like till now, and there's no telling how far it will go, those who've never before suffered will tumble in cascades of their blood, yes I'm telling you, they've already mounted the barricades, though we've not heard them, come twilight they're out there waiting, in the oncoming dark, now almost out in the open, but Fleur's response was, I've got to get back to the hotel by nightfall, and I'll take Su with me, so he can sleep in a real bed at last, what's making him cough like that, he asked, are you trying to kill him, why, but Wrath replied, go on and give him another cigarette, it's too late anyway, to which Fleur protested in defense of a brother, do you want to kill him, no, was Wrath's reply, since no one here will comfort the desolate, I think they should have what they want, and a cigarette is so little to give, poor Su, said Wrath with an air of sincerity that unsettled Fleur, monsters deserve pity too, though we know in this world that pity is sterile, in fact it's non-existent, and while Angel's mother prepared a simple meal for her son, made up mostly of medication washed down with ice cream and fruit, he loved juicy mangoes, apples, and round red cherries, Lena wondered, why am I a mother when I'm going to lose my child, why was I married only for my husband to separate and leave us in misery, why, why, and Angel's on the veranda in a wheelchair, even though I've been shopping, he's barely hungry, he'll be depressed and leave the mangoes on the tray, he's been like that for a while, ever since he got hooked on the cell phone, tablet, social network and all that, none of which interests him any more, he used to be online the minute he got up in the morning, but who would it be with, the virtual world turned not be anything all of a sudden, soon he'd be out of the spotlight, backstage to it all, what news could he give his teenage friends, he wondered, after being kicked out of school, did he even have any friends, except Misha and

Brian, Dr. Dieudonné and Dr. Lorraine, his colleague, came to see him each day, but apart from them, who did he have except his mother, of course, she loved him and was his friend, was it her fault he had no appetite and often had trouble digesting, for he knew his insides were deteriorating like in latent putrefaction, and here she was cutting up his fruit and lifting his head, so he could drink and eat his ice cream, and of course all those pills he had to swallow, did they still work, his mother wondered, Angel too wondered whether they were even a good idea any more, as he watched his life increasingly threatened and limited every day, that's why fainting allowed him the relief of leaving his rotting body, ah, at last, flying out over the galaxies, but his mother and doctors kept their hold on him, each time preventing his escape with resuscitation, you've got to eat to gain strength and courage, Angel, when his body drifted through the clouds, captivated in silence, providential, soundless space containing within it very faint harmonious sounds, as liminal as droplets of water or a voice ushering him closer, closer, a breath of crystal, practically nothing at all and so far off, how to frame it among sounds more familiar, new and unknown detonations, inexplicable yet restful, then balanced with sounds and colours to swim in forever, nothing like the nasty shaking shocks unlike any other when bad spells took hold, no, just the amnesty of silence, Angel's waking sleep, eyelids quivering as he was forced back to his body, stretched out in his wheelchair, sometimes Dr. Dieudonné even ordered him to get up and take a few steps, saying, no, you mustn't give in to this, but as he came back to himself, merely Angel, he could hear their voices closer telling him that he had a family to take care of in Alexandra, South Africa, which had so very few doctors and generations of orphans brought up by their grandmothers for lack of parents, still mistakenly believing it was tuberculosis instead of the scourge they refused to name, while presidents and prime ministers had long feigned ignorance of the secret, yes, the secret, forged ignorance about the deaths of their young parents, young mothers lying emaciated on straw mats nursing infants, dead or in their last throes, influenza perhaps or tuberculosis, said the men who safeguarded this denial, amounting to nothing in areas afflicted with crime and poverty, and the grandmothers went on bringing up the boys and girls of their sons and daughters, thinking as they looked at them in their arms, could it be true that these little ones will leave us as their parents did, aged orphans of them all, and Dr. Dieudonné replied, yes, I understand, I do, but, my dear friend, there is a certain risk in your going back there, and of course I understand your attachment, and look at this boy who almost got away from us once again, oh, here are some visitors for you Angel, and sure enough Angel opened his eyes to see Brilliant and Misha making a racket out on the flower-edged steps leading to the veranda, and he smiled to hear Misha barking and see the wolf-like head as it galloped toward him, while Brilliant said, come on, get up and we'll see the ocean and go out in a boat, okay Angel, so off they went for a few hours, while Angel thought no more of the galaxies and droplets of water in the vastness of unimaginable silence, something he couldn't describe to his mother if he wanted to, though there were times that he tried on his computer, Mama, can you hear the silence of the stars, can you Mama, then he erased it all, maybe he'd merely been dazzled by a dream after all, the suddenness of Bryan and Misha being there, the elderly lady Lucia too, Angel enjoyed the prospect of sailing with Bryan's captain-friend, that Bryan, he had friends everywhere, oh but he wasn't writing enough, Lucia said, and Bryan replied, alright, now you've got to walk like the doctor said, I'll carry you on my back down the gangplank, but not before, c'mon, up and walk, breathe in that air, will you, Angel, his mother Lena came too, and all at once it was so good to be alive, Angel wondered how he could have doubted this, for the child was obviously loved and well surrounded, he wouldn't face the silence of the night and stars alone any more, on shaky legs he followed Bryan racing toward the sea and the sailboat, thinking that soon he would be better, just as Drs. Dieudonné and Lorraine had told him, and his complexion pinked as his mother said, you're such a handsome boy when you laugh, I miss that laughter at home, then she thought of the cloud over his expulsion from school that had enshrouded and defeated them, his father's departure, how could she love a man so weak, but perhaps she was better off raising her son alone, today's moving day, Lucia said, I haven't got much furniture because my sisters took everything, but I've got some lamps, big ones and small ones, I guess you get mindful of them when you've lived without electricity or even a home for months on end, when I came in by the garden in the evening, just a wee bit tipsy perhaps, well, that's how it is when you're with young people like Bryan, it's always party time, either that or drowning one's sorrows, but he's a fine boy just the same, and I love him like a son, well, anyway, the garden was all topsy-turvy, all the lights were out, not a lamp in the place, nothing, I felt the muzzles of my pets, soft and moist, well, I thought, these poor dears need something to drink and eat, but it was so dark, Brilliant, and why did the people from the Shelter come and take them all away, I'd rescued every one of them, why, oh why, Brilliant, do tell me, I haven't many clothes left either, not a single dress any more, I'm going to wear nothing but overalls, and I'll cut my hair real short, then I'll feel freer without all those fripperies, oh not so long ago, I was one of the chiquest women around, I was beautiful, and I designed my own jewelry, but my sisters took the store and all my jewels away from me, oh do you really think I'll finally have a place to stay, my own apartment, one they can't turn me out of, is it really true, Brilliant, then maybe I can get my little ones back, I bet you will, said Brilliant, you'll see your whole menagerie again, but you mustn't ever forget to give them water, Lucia, here you'll have lots and lots of plants too, and your garden will be lit up at night, then Lucia's spirit shone in her eyes, suddenly relieved of all the humiliating persecutions heaped on her, lamps great and small, you need several just in case, though of course the sun is best of all, and I'll have a bicycle too, she beamed at Brilliant, oh and I'll go along the seashore alone and free, she repeated, oh yes, that's how things will be, she pronounced firmly, she said with new vigour but nevertheless fatigued. Fleur spied Su's frail silhouette against the sombre grey of the sky, he held some sort of buttonless overcoat pressed to him, my friends with drums and guitars are waiting on me so we can play till midnight, he said in a broken voice barely audible, holding his lapel against the wind and waving his cigarette with one hand, his fingers trembling on the other, but Wrath stopped him from speaking, isn't it a bit early to leave us, my friend, to go begging in the Metro, singing and playing with your friends, oh what a pity, such a pity that talented musicians like yourselves should be reduced to panhandling, don't you agree Fleur, but Fleur said he'd go with them, Su shouldn't be left alone with a nasty cough like that to wander off to the Metro and climb the stairs to where his rock-group was, no, said Fleur, we're not doing that, Su was pale already, and walking might bring on a fainting-spell, he's so pale, and that cough really, he said, then Wrath surprised him with an icy ironic laugh, look at you now, playing shepherd to a lost lamb who can only wander farther away than he has already, back when I was in charge of souls, I loved the Good Shepherd of the gospels and even compared myself to him, that was before I lost my reason of course, yet still sometimes when I'm asleep or pretend to be — among my flock, the flea-bitten denizens of the tunnels — or lie down, dusty and filthy, on top of my oversize shadow, itself in the gloom of the Supreme Shadow which looms over all, I still dream of those in my care at the start of my ecclesiastical career, and no, I wasn't only counting uncounted sheep but children, orphans I revisited in my dreams, for yes, I do still carry some of them on my shoulders and others in my large, welcoming arms, all of them so slight, almost transparently pale from malnutrition, weighing so very little, perhaps not enough to survive, still I promised them a cure, a home somewhere forever free of privation, and together we walked as they clutched the folds of my clothing, or held onto the billowing flesh of my neck as we walked toward the far-off and shining kingdom of the city, but all of a sudden I don't know where they are, have they fallen from my arms, did I, misbegotten, trample them, I call out to them long and loud, but nothing comes back, they're simply gone, and I'll never see them again, then I wake up feeling as though I'm carrying iron bars in my arms, gone are my orphans, Wrath said, why oh why is it, he asked Su, wrapped in his black overcoat, oh I know all, Su, I really do, your quest to the Beanpole is for your nightly cocaine, my poor lamb, and the echo came back in Su's cough, thought Fleur, we mustn't let him go, he exclaimed, no, absolutely not, Brilliant gazed at those he called his little family, his world opening out into the whole of humanity at last, with a tender glance toward Lucia, Lena, Angel — looking more tanned in the setting sun — hey Beanpole Brilliant, called out the captain as he manoeuvred his sailboat on a sea that looked a little too turbulent to Brilliant, so you've finally brought us back Misha, hey, Joe the Giant, nice boat you have here, got any champagne for us, boy lotta waves this evening, nope, me and Misha won't ever be apart again, never, Brilliant yelled to his friend as the boat waltzed on the waves, Joe yelled back, I saw in the papers the town's giving you an award, one of the five Top Volunteers at the Acacia Gardens, bringing them meals in their rooms, I'd never expected that from you, quite an honour, excellence in volunteering, how about that Beanpole Bryan, I admit I was wrong when I thought you'd be just one more long-term drunk hanging out in the bars and fishermen's taverns, my friends would like some of your champagne too, Bryan yelled back, say how did you manage to buy a sailboat like this, Joe the Giant sailor, one of these days I'll tell you, came back the answer, yep, later, in private, you still involved in shady deals, Joe, same old adventuring buccaneer as always, eh Joe, that too I'll tell you about that later as well, but congrats on the Gardens and all, Beanpole, I'm real pleased, but we won't be seeing each other too often, I'm off to the Bahamas, Panama too, got business down there, what kind, said Bryan, I'll explain later, said Joe, got to find your own way in life, don't you, jeez Beanpole, who'd've thought eh, Top Volunteer, and that was when Brilliant worried about Angel being seasick as he leaned out over the waves with his mother's hand on his shoulder, though he'd loved it all, with the dolphins dancing right beside them, nah, he wouldn't be sick, Brilliant thought, I'm so happy, he recalled the town's award for the past few months of taking hot meals with added vitamins up to house-bound residents at the Gardens who, not long ago, had been going out amid gangs of young people at night, visiting the Porte du Baiser Saloon on the sly with its green sauna often before dawn, united in their illness and the unnameable thing that was getting steadily closer, they went out feeling shrunken and pressed together, fewer and fewer of them, friends, buddies, thought Brilliant sadly, till there were only two or three of them left, what a pity, he thought, for he loved them all, and how painful when one was no longer there waiting, ghosts of themselves behind the screen door, was it bearable even before that, when one of them approached leaning on a cane, or another tried to conceal his blindness with his hand, or their sudden stupefying thinness despite being so young, or the hot meals gradually forgotten and spoiled as each apartment emptied one after another, he felt Misha's huge head on his face, ah, he had his wolf back, cured of the traumas he'd suffered in the hurricanes, we're lucky, aren't we Mischa, we're so happy now, well, except for Pirate Joe being too stingy to dip into his cases of champagne or offer us a cool beer when we're so thirsty, it would be nice, wouldn't it Mischa, Petites Cendres was running more slowly down Atlantic Boulevard, as he remembered Robbie's coronation as the 25th drag queen one night, beginning onstage, then the first dance in the street, when Robbie had said all the profits tonight are for The Acacia Gardens and medical research, and what a hit it was, Robbie got a round of applause from the party-goers who were drunk on rum, and Mabel, with Jerry the parrot on her shoulder, had sold all her ginger-and-lemon drinks, oh what a night Robbie's coronation was, he thought, a carnival, that's what, with Herman under his orange wig there for the last time, never to get up from the bed in the house his mother had rented for him nearby, all so he wouldn't have far to walk to the Saloon, Jerry sitting on her shoulder asking Mabel where Merlin was, Mama, where's Merlin Mama, while men who'd been drunk since noon danced all around them they parroted Jerry, singing, *Mama, where is Merlin, tell me Mama, and give us a drink Mama, but not that ginger stuff Mabel,* she stood up for her parrot, saying, sure so you can throw up all over the place you no-goods, you put us all to shame, and later that evening, Robbie and Petites Cendres laid eyes on the bar-stools where Yinn had painted celebrity faces like Herman, Fatalité and the others, then he heard a woman's voice and thought of Herman, at first he didn't recognize her, youthful and svelte in a black summer dress, but, yes, there she was, Herman's mother, looking tenderly at Petites Cendres and asking how he was, and why they so rarely saw him at the Saloon, what's wrong, those green eyes he'd seen in Herman settled on him with the very same gaze, penetrating Petites Cendres' outer shell of solitude, she said there hadn't been enough time to think through her mourning with two teenagers still at home, and she'd needed to find a job, she spoke simply, and it was as if she'd slipped into

Herman's place at the Cabaret, helping the girls with their makeup, sometimes taking over from Yinn's mother at the ticket counter, she even got involved in the shows with Yinn as if he were her son, refreshing his image every night, that's how she explained it to Petites Cendres, as though she and Herman had never parted, she was voluble but serene as she solemnly laid her hand on the seat decorated with Herman's face, the fleshy lips seeming to say, you see, I'm with you after all and for a good long time, my friends, Petites Cendres meanwhile pictured the child-size bed in the rented house, where Herman's breathing had suddenly stopped and his gaze became fixed, with Yinn lying on top of him and yelling, you're stoned, just stoned, you wake up right now Herman, all of them standing around the bed in their gaudy flowered dresses and voluminous blonde wigs, which had slid forward just a bit in the midst of all this emotion and excitement, all of them standing there, Geisha, Santa Fe, Heart Triumphant, and Know-It-All, tears running with their Rimmel mascara, not a breath, said Yinn, not a breath, I hear nothing, and he massaged Herman's chest, no, there's nothing, then Herman's mother suddenly spoke up, you're all wrapped up in your thoughts, you mustn't think about it too much, as long as I'm alive, my son will be alive in me, you know, she told Petites Cendres later, every evening I show them videos of him singing and dancing, in all kinds of places, Mexico, Provincetown, and there will always be applause and laughter when he gets provocative, he hated all that was stupid you know, and ignorance, oh, he loved taking pokes at that and surprising people, I guess in his own way, he was trying to get people to change somehow, like his mother, I didn't get it at first, every mother worries about her son I guess, but I don't any more, he's at peace now, I know that, it's better not to think about those things, you know Petites Cendres, and back in the present, he trotted slowly, thinking he heard her voice and felt Herman's gaze slide down his neck, you've gotta get stronger, run faster, Herman was saying, he really had to finish his book *Strange Years*, thought Daniel, interminable, unfinished and impossible, noticing among all the rich and detailed events, he'd included the last moment of the lizard, fixed like a diamond pinned to a wall so it sparkled all the more, but the book was already too full of things, too coloured with words, fleeting impressions and memories, as though coming to light only then and there, the little lizard, or the appearance of snails on the doorstep after a warm rain was part of what had been, not what would be, at least he hadn't crushed the snails, staring down at them just in time, then bending to set them aside on the wood planks along with a bowl of water for Mai's cats, knowing the two of them didn't get along, but that they'd still manage to share, he hadn't dared re-read the five hundred pages he'd written in the past few days and nights, while Mélanie and the kids weren't around, kids, he had to remind himself they weren't there any more, no, their rooms would stay empty in the coming weeks, he could ramble disappointed through their emptiness saying the whole bunch would be back any day, or at least for the summer holidays, though with them nothing was certain, might as well admit it, and next week his wife would be back from her conferences in Russia, and he'd go out and fetch her from the airport, but she'd be the only one arriving, not his turbulent sons, and all he could do was think of Vincent and Samuel, not so much Augustino though, who rarely sent any news, it would have to wait for Mai's graduation, otherwise there'd be no one, not even Samuel who barely a few years ago still jumped into the pool from the second floor with a flash of his red trunks, his mother wasn't too happy about that, Daniel recalled, and here he was, Samuel the New York choreographer, no longer the wily boy in the red trunks, hardly even the same son, apparently banished by another version of himself, and Mai, well, she'd left her cats and dogs in the care of Mélanie and Daniel, and at least this animal extension of her into the present gave Daniel some comfort, and he knew that if Mai came back home, it would be because she missed them if not him, she never wrote her father, oh how I miss you, but she mentioned every animal by name, saying she couldn't live without them, still they wouldn't be allowed on the campus, how are they, were they eating alright, she asked her father, and often that was all she talked about, you had to read between the lines to decode the affection she had for her parents, or at least whatever was left of it, that's the way it was with Mai, scraps that a father like Daniel survived on, this description had made its way into his book with a click on her screen-face, piercings and all, the blue screen brought her to life for him, the click made or broke the spell, but her presence in the book was indelible, echoed in the flood of last night's words and phrases, obscure and timid, capable of insolence, even violence, so complex was this work, the ultimate challenge of expressing himself fully, but not quite, words written as though he'd spoken and broken the silence he preferred, despite this silence of the house often hospitable to him without them all, Mélanie as well as the children, though the evening before he'd invited Charles and Frédéric, yet here he was, climbing the green steps to the wooden house for the first time since Frédéric's death and funeral, no wait, it was Charles's wasn't it, one had followed the other so closely, love seemed to have drawn them sacredly together even in this, Charles had willed the house to the city to be used by young poets and novelists to come and write, how incredible it was for this future projection to be planted firmly in the present, for Charles had seen it as a dream in the distant future, not right away, Daniel went in and shook the hand of the young New York novelist who lived there at present, fortunately an ardent admirer of Charles and his books, and it seemed almost the same as before, even if Charles and Frédéric were no longer there, you know, the younger man said offering a hash-joint to Daniel, an elegant gesture like any other in a house so unlike any other, it feels as though Charles and Frédéric are still here, especially Frédéric, nestled in one of these wicker armchairs, watching us in ironic mockery and saying, why here they come to visit us, Daniel mentioned that Frédéric had a particular, slightly negligent way of holding himself, looking at people cheek-on-fist with a lock of hair over his laughing eye, more like a wing really, the wing of a pigeon or a dove, he said, there was definitely something angelic about Frédéric, well, benevolent and almost angelic anyway, he continued, as though Frédéric were really there with him, lecturing him for being unduly modest about his books, you have no self-confidence, my dear Daniel, like me from the time I was young and never touched the piano again, at fifteen or sixteen, I was in some concert-hall in Los Angeles, when I sensed the envious gaze of my younger brother, jealous to the point of madness, so I decided that the virtuoso wasn't going to be me any more, I couldn't do it, continuing to play would have been like killing him,

Daniel, no, I simply couldn't do it, hurt my brother with feelings like that, and that same day I said goodbye to a career in music, Daniel was hearing this voice again where it had lived with Charles for so long, painting and writing, the Greek pictures still on the walls breathed the sweet air of Athens, with blue skies and a few white clouds forming, he explained to the young writer that he didn't smoke any more, not since he got married and had kids, it was pretty pretentious advertising his wisdom like that, or was it merely moderation creeping into his former bad habits, Daniel wondered as he sat in Frédéric's wicker chair observing the young novelist Stephen lighting a hash-pipe with something stronger in it this time that made him cough, he said, I don't do this every day, only since I came to this island full of temptation everywhere, and just as he said this, another young man came in without a word to Daniel, abruptly told Stephen he was going out for dinner, oh, um, I thought we were going together, said the novelist, that was Eli, he said as the young man left, he's from the North, and he's travelled around by boat a lot, other than that, I don't know anything about him, except he came by a few days ago to help me close a window that opened onto a palm-tree with rats nesting in it, only palm-rats of course, but that window had to be closed, your friends weren't bothered by this sort of thing, I know, but I am, it beats me how they could paint, write and throw all those parties, especially a great poet like Charles, I really don't get it, but Daniel was thinking that this Eli, even though he only briefly showed up in the living room without even saying hello before leaving again, didn't appeal to him at all, almost as though an aura of danger followed him, suddenly as though Frédéric were speaking through him, he said, don't hang around with him, he's not good for you or this house, then Stephen said, why he came to upset things here, or what drew him to me, I don't know, but his beauty is inspiring, don't you think, I've hardly ever seen such a handsome boy, but Daniel repeated, don't hang around with him, that's all, well, Stephen replied, he said he was clean, no more heroin, all done, and he wasn't lying, at least, I don't believe so, but Daniel persisted, saying that Stephen knew nothing about this Eli, and Daniel had a presentiment that the acquaintance could turn out to be disastrous, during the minutes they held this discussion, he felt as though Frédéric brushed him attentively with an angel-wing, warning him, standing guard on the young novelist and his house against the other young man, who, though he might have the beauty of a devil, carried a world of treachery and most dangerous secrets, an altogether disagreeable feeling, though Daniel could not figure out why, he who was so rarely suspicious, or was he still subject to the writer's hallucinations, absorbed in a dream about Eli that he couldn't put into a book, so unfamiliar to him was the utterly perverse, that was it, Eli exuded an insidious and immoral perversity, one might have said he was here to steal Frédéric's paintings right off the wall, make away with very soul of the house, his cold, blue eyes casting a spell over the young novelist all the while, for not only would he get no writing done while the visitor was here, but he was utterly devastated by this spell, giving way under Eli's tutelage to a latent addiction that would destroy him by degrees, but then, Daniel thought, perhaps the novelist in him was simply building this tragedy around Stephen, but what tragedy might he, in turn, be building around Daniel, thinking what a bore these timid writers from past generations must be, never daring to take a risk, thus the two observed and gauged one another seated face-to-face on Frédéric and Charles's wicker chairs, dressed in similar jeans and unbuttoned white shirts, suntanned and barefoot in sandals, though of course, as Daniel reflected, he was old enough to be Stephen's father, Stephen was Samuel's age, about thirty, and as he inhaled his hash, he probably thought of Daniel as just another old preacher of morality, a writer of faded, outmoded feelings, while Stephen, bearer of the true fire, was consumed in a blaze of the senses by every desire he encountered, even those he steered clear of himself. Thus ran Daniel's thoughts as he visited the home of Charles and Frédéric willed to future writers, such as the current one, Stephen, who — along with the seductive and implacable demon Eli — made their way into Daniel's book *Strange Years*, perhaps he'd seen something of his past self in Stephen, he so wanted to save someone from self-immolation by drugs, and Eli would waste no time offering him heroin and enmeshing him in its net of dependency, how far it would lead, thought Daniel, for Stephen, confused, foggy, no longer able to write, had already confided to Daniel his recent experiment with an old drug, LSD, a very pure sample provided by a chemist friend, and one night he'd awoken terrified from hearing steps in the desert then close behind him like loud bells, I'm telling you Daniel, I was terrified by the sound of my own feet, and the desert was endless, burning hot, and filled with scorpions, you know how I hate those things, and Eli tells me there are some in the garden here, snakes too, explain to me how your distinguished friends could survive in a wild place like this, I dream of them at night because of the drugs, walking in the desert among these scorpions, and Eli with his cold eyes and sinister beauty, all this Stephen stored away as matter for his book as he said to Daniel, this is what we write, isn't it, what obsesses us in such uncontrolled fever, all the while, Daniel reproached his own tepid writing, neither feverish nor toxic, how was it possible to be so normal and still write so much, surely more obsessed and hallucinatory than he thought, and how could he write so raw, so un-ornamentally, when Stephen, surely a genuine writer of the abyss, was unadapted to living, while Daniel adored every instant of life, even if it meant not seeing his children for long periods, this was his dependence, he concluded, Mai said it too, he loved them too much, and what afflicted him most was the disconcerting insolence of Augustino, he felt similar to Stephen ditched for supper by Eli, off to see another man, and Daniel, like Stephen, put up with these affronts, pardoned them, what choice did they really have if they wanted to see those they loved again, as proud as he was, Stephen the dandy would often be baffled, while Daniel patiently waited for the day he would see his son, and as Daniel wrote all his stories, multiple and multiplying, he must omit the rats in the palms, the scorpions and snakes that so frightened Stephen, all the things that never bothered Charles and Frédéric in their gardens, or perhaps they'd never noticed, except for the day Caroline killed one with her shoe on the wood floor of the living room, that annoyed Frédéric, who reproached her, Caroline, no one hurts anyone here, but she replied, it was either the scorpion or Jean-Mathieu's foot, that's where it was headed, yes, Frédéric said, but so slowly, and you know it's hardly more than a bee-sting, is that a reason to kill them like that, you see, said Stephen, Charles, and Frédéric lived in comfort with the scorpions and snakes they never even noticed in their garden, this note of Stephen's would also find its way into Daniel's book, and as he continually expanded it this way, altering the structure as it opened itself wider and wider, there was a movement of encroaching reality as hard to control as a horse in fury, the past spilling out from behind the fragile silhouette of Stephen and his hash, or writing here in Charles's study — all of it, Olivier, Chouan and their son Jermaine; Caroline and Jean-Mathieu with their political divergences — where he could still hear their discussions, sometimes quite sharp, all of them present, including Mélanie and the children, young at the time, plus Daniel himself in the first pangs of fatherhood, he came to fear the writing would be too intractable, but was it writing or fatherhood that was so hard, what did he know back then, consumed with his own desires, just like Stephen now, though lacking the same ambition, yes all of them were present that evening to celebrate the reissuing of Justin's book condemning the destruction of Hiroshima, which was popular with students, though it had its detractors, was this the same night Daniel wondered if Caroline was one of those, but saying nothing to avoid hurting Justin, though her expression betrayed her, and suddenly she'd said to those who were listening that in those war-years, women had risen to new heights due to the patriotic effort, why she herself had learned to fly, then Jean-Mathieu distracted her by coming near, and she fell silent once more, as Justin spoke up, a pastor's son brought up in China, Daniel recalled him saying, what was it, ah yes, in this undertaking of war we mis-identify the murderous racism we are capable of in the madness we undertake, that most of all is what I wanted to get across in the book, and in saying so, Justin had brought a curious tension into Caroline's face, then came Jean-Mathieu's awkward approach to her, I have experienced how refined these peoples are, Justin went on, so how could I possibly take part in such massacres, really, how could I, then his voice dissolved into the hubbub of celebration, that and a crystal glass broken by three-year-old Samuel, scolded and crying in Mélanie's arms, it was Daniel that scolded him and Mélanie that comforted him, paternal severity versus maternal indulgence, too quick to punish a child's clumsiness, and Frédéric said, no crying Samuel, there's plenty of time for tears when you are grown, and they'll come all by themselves, then he took Samuel in his arms, everyone saying how cute he looked in his woollen outfit on that cool January evening, Daniel still blamed himself for those sobs, thinking he'd scolded the boy too severely, much too strongly, as Mélanie said when the evening was done, the past was oozing out everywhere as Daniel kept writing, even those tears he thought he'd forgotten but which shamed him now. And Mick had always known other students would join his Pact Against Hate, no need to hide out on the roof of Trinity College with his banner any more, there were other boys and girls going from class to class with him carrying signs and unmistakeable close-ups of students who had disappeared after being bullied or beaten, as though a continuous wave carried them off every day to another world, young suicides, Mick thought, and here they were again, breathing, revived in the smiles they wore when photographed, never doubting the future would betray them with its final brutality and their inevitable-seeming suicides, so, said Mick at each of the meetings and speeches he gave, is that what you want for yourselves, or your sister, or your brother, he showed them the pictures of Tyler, a promising violinist you'll never ever hear, because he drowned himself; this is William; that's Asher; here's Set, do you want your sister jumping off a bridge like Tyler, or hanging herself in a barn at age thirteen, would you, eh, and in fright they listened, pitiful and entranced, some timidly siding with Mick's friends, saying, yes, I want to be part of this, but the bigger ones'll gang up on me, I already had to let them take my watch and iPhone, another one was crying on Mick's shoulder and saying he was afraid for his life, they'd threatened him, and Mick saw the wounds on his neck and signs of molestation that made him think of his sister Tammy, who never left the house any more for being anorexic and persecuted, they called her The Corpse, trundled from clinic to clinic so she could learn to eat again, she wanted to look like a model, Mick thought, poisoned by disappointment in herself and her body, self-mutilating, and here was Mick saying, would you like to have this happen to you, and so the numbers of the Alliance Against Hate multiplied, and Mick preached from under cover no more, not since learning karate and freeing himself from a fence the monsters had nailed him to, and now he felt the strength to protect himself and those who were defenseless against terror and intimidation, and all this while, Tammy was in the hands of her nurses, and when she did get home emaciated, she dared not go out, not to college, not to see her friends, for she had none, or so she thought, and all that awaited her was intolerance and intimidation, so why go out at all, here in the house her writer parents forgot all about her, didn't even notice her, now, all of a sudden, they had other concerns than taking care of a child who was rapidly running downhill in self-denigration, was it even a sickness, no, better not talk about it, more like a congenital degeneration really, the disgrace of an intellectual family, her father a renowned historian, and a writer mother who considered both her children as obstacles, Tammy never read any of her mother's books, though Mick did, searching for the slightest clue that his mother loved him a bit, despite it all, he told himself a mother's love was something basic and animal, they were so alike with identical gestures and vocal inflections, as though Mick were more her daughter than her son, and there was the problem, he was more girl-like than boyish, the coolest daring looks, but how was Tammy going to get through this, he wondered, she used to have Mai as a friend, but she was a healthy girl not subject to underrating herself or silent and suicidal the way Tammy was, and after a while she'd inevitably been pushed away, how else could it be in such disorientated uncertainty, Mick on the other hand, was no longer alone, though still busy with his enemies, one having yelled at him when he showed his placards of young suicides to a meeting, one day it's your sister The Corpse we're gonna see up there, yeah, that's the one, the retard, this really got to Mick, but looking round at fellow members of his Alliance raised his hopes again, and knowing he wasn't alone, rocked by the waves as the boat made for the marina, Brilliant was declaiming his reunion with Misha, of course Lucia, sipping her glass of red wine, had heard it so many times she wasn't listening, so Angel was his only captive audience, and he laughed again upon hearing that Mischa was a canine citizen with all the rights of a real one, the story of Mischa being the story of many dogs that survived the First and Second Great Devastations, Brilliant's voice sang out over the waves as he leaned on the gunwhale of the boat with his hair flying, refuges were filled with these poor animals all along the Gulf Coast and in all the pounds on the Mississippi, what a panicked clamour when the cages closed on them, some had spent three days in volunteer trucks, O blessed be them that saved you Mischa, you and those four Spaniels, no more than pups when the waters rose and houses buckled, dogs wandering hungry and thirsty, families of survivors still there for some of them, though their houses had no walls, and in the enormity of it all, cats and dogs also clung to ruins till the helicopter came and the brave pilot took us along with the Spaniels and an Eskimo dog, but Mischa had an ear infection from the water that scrambled his brains and cuts beneath his fur, how long it had taken him to recover, yet here he is alive and well there at your feet, exclaimed Angel, for this was the ultimate truth of Brilliant's sometimes shadowy tale, Misha could survive just about anything, take a look at those ears pricked up, free of infection, and his wolfish teeth, lesions cured, and so full of the joy of life, proof against misfortune, so perhaps one day Misha's miracle would also lead Angel to recovery under the spell of his admired friend's eloquence, okay just a bit crazy maybe, they said Billiant was cracked since the hurricanes, now adding Angel's story to his declamations, a narrative of struggle after struggle, but no, Angel's thoughts stopped at the charm of it all, with no particular ending in mind, and what a beautiful history it would make, it really is a pity he doesn't write it all down, Lucia said, he recites only what he doesn't write, the boat bobbed toward the port, where the others were tied up at the marina near a sandy beach where, as if by some mysterious word-of-mouth, the low-flying pelicans and the turtle-doves, flying low over the sidewalks, all gathered, Lucia suddenly fell prey to concerns about her sisters, as well as the keys she was busy searching for in her cluttered handbag before entering her dark house from a dark garden followed by the noses of pets as lost and hungry as she, though that was her own fault for having forgotten to eat breakfast or lunch, oh dear, she was forgetting everything lately, she could have shared a meal with Brilliant instead of only drinking while they laughed and had fun in the bars, really it was her own fault if her sisters were hostile and the bills kept coming into her mailbox never to be paid, she really should have said something to Brilliant, then they wouldn't have cut off her electricity and heating in the winter cold, she trudged through the dried piles of palm-leaves, the garden was such a mess, that too was her fault, there was a hole, a blank space in her memory these days, blank as the dark house, humidity starting to smell like rot, so she lay don on the floor, no point in getting undressed tonight, a night smelling of alcohol, the solitude of her body on the floor, naked among the vermin, oh no, her sisters mustn't discover her like this in the morning, they'd say she was crazed, no, not tonight, she'd sleep in a clean bed at the Acacia Gardens, with no one to torment her and throw her out, Brilliant had promised he'd pay the bills for her, and tonight would be different, Lucia thought, she'd be in heaven. The boats seemed empty as they slid along the water in a thick grey fog, it'll soon be night, Wrath said to Fleur, holding him captive without moving a muscle, a monument of shadow in the rough outline of an overcoat next to the boy and Su, while the old woman in scarves sniffed around Fleur, hey Young Man, she said pinching his arm, don't forget to give me a little something before you go, a little reward, y'know, sure you're going, I'm certain of that, besides if you get stuck here, Wrath'll destroy you, he always does when he brings someone under a bridge, look at Su, he's finished, they all are, yet once again Wrath violently pushed her away, hey what about Tai, she yelled as he threw her up against a brick wall, what have you done with Tai, eh Wrath, old witch, he shot back, seems to me I saw you once burning at the stake in the time of the Holy Inquisition when they burned heretics and sorcerers like you, yes, the time of our Supreme Jurisdiction, you criminal with your witchcraft, oh how I'd love to be part of the ecclesiastical courts that punished and burned everything in their path, who knows, maybe I actually was there in those glorious courts of ours, you know I hate women, don't you Old Witch, they want to take over the Inquisition from us, pull our laws out from under us, but what they really want is to control us, and when we deflower their daughters and sons, they're hot on our trail, they are the real Inquisition snooping around in our morals, our secret pleasures stolen from the innocents, as Tai used to tell me with contempt from up high on his moral pedestal, we wouldn't know what to do with them anyway, Wrath you're just a merchant, a trader in infant flesh, soft as silk, a greed-merchant, piling up whatever you can, aren't you Wrath, that's what the miserable, insolent Tai said to me, I bought him directly from his very own parents in a Bangkok bordello, yes, that's right, he took that liberty, and I listened to his insolent tirade without saying a word, I always felt sorry for his misery, shivering away like that in his overcoat, then Su broke in, my friends are waiting for me in the Metro, and you're just raving anyway Wrath, maybe feverish like me in this weather, yep, they're waiting for me, his barely audible voice murmured in broken accents whipped away by the wind, a whiff of flowers out over the water, a delicious spring smell, Fleur thought, they all had flower-names in that whorehouse, Wrath said, Tai was a rose almost blown, not long before he was mine, intoxicating with the sweet contempt on his lips, while I offered him all manner of delights in return, everything he wanted, spoiled, they all want to be spoiled, stuffed like infants after they've gone days without eating, they're everywhere, you know, Tai, his brothers, his sisters, literally everywhere, of course Tai was right, I bargained for them with some disgusted, furtive fellow in a floating market where they begged in front of the Buddhist temples in Thornburi, Tai used to steal shoes from the tourists or else go begging in squats, grabbing their legs as though in play on their filthy, repugnant beds, toying with them behind curtains of fake pearls, I used to cut a fairly gallant, somewhat majestic figure in those days, and they recognized me right away for the priest disguised as a merchant, the treachery I kept hidden, ah, who'd've known me then, Fleur, eh, but like every leacherous trader, I got too confident, and I made the mistake of taking Tai to Europe with me, and this bold, condescending boy was going to betray me out of sheer hatred for what he called my hideousness, oh he said it many times as we crossed Europe by train, it does pain me to see that hateful shadow again, every bit of his shamed and injured hate, yes, I still see it, I do, in stations at morning and night time, Tai, and what did you do to Tai under those bridges, inquired the drunk-voiced Old Woman from under her scarves, eh Wrath, what did'ja do, he removed his hat as though to dismiss her, then put it back over his tangled hair, saying to Fleur, don't listen to her, how's an old man to hide a child in an international airport these days, but with Tai it was no problem, a teen and tall for his age, no problem at all, my adopted son was everything to me, rescued from beggarliness, my link with Asia, and how's a portly man going to hide a kid on a train, yet there he was, by my side, forever trailing his shadow of hate, oh it cut me to the soul, all I could know of love was the suffering, nothing more, and his refusal of me put ice in my veins, so many risks I'd taken, yet to be so hatefully despised, I dressed him well so he looked a bit like me, more civilized, I still remember his clenched jaw with white teeth that looked about to tear off strips of my flesh, though his smile gave no hint at all of his detestation, the sort of contempt a slave would have, you know what I mean, Fleur, and then everything became terrifying, he had some shady connections to men in power, and when he turned me in or was on the point of it, I had no choice, none, well, he awakened violent feelings in me, every bit as violent as his own, ah then what did you do to him, the Old Woman cried with a voice that cut through the river-fog, what did you do to Tai, I had to make a decision, said Wrath with a lowered voice and drained face which gave Su the shivers that had nothing to do with the cold, Tokyo, he said, my mother and my wife are waiting for me, it'll only be a few weeks yes, just a few, he said in a breaking voice that was barely audible. Since introducing Eli into his book, Daniel began seeing him everywhere, when he was out walking Mai's dogs on Bahama Street, he thought he spied him, so rarely with his host Stephen the novelist that he seemed like an impostor, almost always alone, then suddenly near the public pool on Bahama chatting with some black kids who bought his drugs, there always seemed to be a cloud of duplicity surrounding him, a soul as two-sided as his face, hypocrisy veiled in a gentle look, what exactly did he expect from his illicit doings with such young boys and girls at his mercy, humiliating them with the white man's disdain perhaps, or recognizing in them the same thugs he once saw in himself, this pool had been built by Isaac, Daniel's uncle, dug as a protest against the racism and segregation undergone by black children who'd once been refused admission to city beaches, it seemed so long ago to Daniel and his family, but not to Pastor Jérémie and his children, Venus, Carlos, and their brothers and sisters, whom Daniel remembered so well, it seemed like yesterday Venus and Samuel had sung together, *oh abiding joy, oh abiding joy* when they were twelve and in love, coming home from school together, their arms round each other's shoulder, maybe Venus was just a few years older than Samuel, but they had sung together at the Temple du Corail, surely a miracle of life that can't be destroyed, thought Daniel, yes, there was Uncle Isaac's pool with its young bathers from Esmeralda Street, an arch of marble over the water as though reaching for some irreconcilable union, a meeting of the races, a meeting or reunion suspended for oh so long, as Isaac had said the day it was inaugurated, I believe we'll never be forgiven, and why should we, it revolted Daniel to see Eli there, not far from the pool his uncle had built as a tribute to racial harmony, Eli in all his handsome shadiness, his lies and secrets, risky offerings to children whose ancestors who had suffered so much abuse and injustice, when a young female swimming instructor chased him off, though not suspicting him of anything in paricular, still he felt unwelcome and went away down parallel streets to other parts, the young woman had simply wanted to talk to him, that was Eli, thought Daniel, capable of deflecting suspicion, affable, polite, and innocent-looking, capable of concealment in a group of kids, one of them, just as harmless, though Daniel knew better, the twisted secrets behind his flight like sudden apparitions, and sometimes at nightfall after Suzanne's death, Daniel dined with Adrien at the Grand Hotel, when all of a sudden there was Eli in the lobby, apparently waiting for someone, friend or client, always dressed with refinement, a stylish, informal look he might have learned from Stephen, who was never there at such moments to join him for the evening or have a walk by the sea, maybe a cocktail, no, there were always other men, often older than Stephen and of indefinable origin, vaguely marbinal despite meeting in the lobby, his social world thus took on a mysterious aura, and it annoyed Daniel, what was he doing here, everywhere in fact, but here in the hotel imagined and built by Isaac for artists and writers, a place for rest and meditation with salons named for painters and writers, with bookshelves in all of them, with a piano in the centre, surrounded by large white-curtained windows open to the ocean, it had changed owners several times, no longer the calm retreat it once was, but still the comfy salons where Daniel joined Adrien, not the best of friends, it was the memory of Suzanne that drew Daniel and the irritable writer to one another, Adrien having roasted Augustino's books while toasting his father's, seeing Adrien in his white trousers and navy jacket, Daniel could still hear him laughing about the boy's books as though his review were right there in front of him, no, Daniel appreciated the older man's culture and learning, but not the man himself, the kind that for whatever reason, possibly mean-spirited envy, would love to demolish

Augustino, and perhaps he'd succeeded, though his son was resilient and went on publishing, yet both men had loved the same woman, Suzanne, and Daniel could truly share the loss that left Adrien inconsolable, and it was always with her in mind that they saw one another, literature — especially Augustino's work — was left in silence, something they both disliked, but that was how it had to be, thought Daniel, one had to like and respect the crusty older man's life with a woman who had surrounded him in her light. With a brusque gesture, Adrien got up from his spacious armchair and impatiently said, why waste time here in the Emerson and Thoreau rooms so Isaac's Romanticism will lull us with nostalgia for past writers, what good is it, they're gone after all, and here we are still among the living, come on, let's go outside in the sun by the sea, dear Daniel, come, you know Suzanne and I watched you grow up, then your own children, dear Suzanne, he said again, his eyes moistening under the white African hat, believe me, if I linger much longer on this earth, I'll be as old and decrepit as your uncle Isaac, what an undying grace in living that man has, still planning and creating too, building that tower-house of his looking out over the ocean on the Island No One Owns, and do you know, he still manages to climb all those steps toward the blue sky, and there he contemplates his restful eternity, and down below amid the wild grasses, the Florida Panther he'll no doubt manage to save, all those little foxes too, and so many other species he'll leave to students, in a word, my dear Daniel, your uncle is king, in those same old khaki shorts and walking with a cane, however modest, he is inhabited by a regal spirit, and that's our Isaac, he was born poor, very poor, and he'll never be like others as rich as he, ah, the wind's cooler here by the ocean, every day my deckchair waits for me here by the quay, came Daniel, let's chat a bit more, right here is where I look to my Faust each day, the second volume I mean, wherein I approach the tormenting question of the devil's grip on our lives, then he suddenly fell silent, remembering that Daniel really shouldn't still be there beside him when Charly came in the limo to run errands, they'd dine somewhere together, but Daniel shouldn't be present till then, or was it just a dream that Charly served him, like the waiter he offered a tip to, pretending to be a resident of the Grand Hotel, it was pleasant for a poet to dream of a place like this among the palms, water fountains and shimmering pools, particularly when he reflected on his solitude, despite his demanding cleaning lady Dorothea, the story-teller he'd taught to write, and on the verge of doing it as well as he, though she was obsessed with tales from the Bible, the only thing she read for now, but at least with her he was never wholly alone, the house with no Suzanne in it did seem lonely, no Suzanne writing behind her Japanese screen, no Suzanne who . . . then he remembered his dream, within which he'd nevertheless felt the irritation of insomnia, so he dreamed he wasn't asleep, not last night, nor tonight, he even heard himself complain about it, when oh when can I get some sleep, and unseen, Suzanne said, dear Adrien, come and lie down by me in the green shade, and we'll sleep together, and he had no idea how he had slept beside her, confident, unhesitating, and now when he thought of this dream, he told himself she must be somewhere in the house watching over him, on the other side of the Japanese screen, yes, his dear Suzanne, then at once, he noticed Daniel was gone, why had he left so quickly, for once Adrien hadn't pestered him with distasteful criticism of Augustino's books, in fact he'd even intended to say something nice about them, there was just no understanding that man, Daniel was really too touchy when it came to his children, pity, he could turn out to be a friend one of these days, fairly soon, they didn't have all that long to wait, Adrien opened his notebook on his lap to the poem "Giving Account", though he knew it by heart, slipped in among his notes for Volume II on Faust, perhaps he'd need to give account of friendships lost or mangled, mismanaged or misbegotten because of his cantankerous nature, why not just admire the colours of the sunset over the sea instead, and since it was cocktail hour, he ordered one with ice, don't forget the ice, he'd tell the waiter with an air of authority. This cough of Su's out in the fog rising off the river at night, it brought back to Fleur all those unpleasant memories as night crept on and through near-deserted streets, people encrusted in the cardboard that separated them from garbage cans and settling in with the paper and rubbish, their feet sticking out onto the sidewalk, knowing they were invisible, not inaudible, Jérôme the African coughing and grousing hoarsely, trying to roll himself in cardboard sheets that were too small for his large body, okay so let's go sleep in sticky wet paper, he yelled, it's raining on the beach tonight, he went on shouting and coughing, envelopes sticking to your skin, that's all the tents we've got tonight, thought Fleur, a bed of leftovers, yelled Jérôme from his cardboard box wedged between two garbage cans, Kim and Fleur embarrassed at being pushed together, what would his mother think if she saw him now, under an avalanche of waste, sleeping in a box with Kim, and barefoot on the wet sidewalk, with their dogs to watch over them, ready to bite whoever came too close, you could hear them growling, you had to wonder what Fleur's mother Martha would think seeing him and hearing Su's fatal-sounding cough as he got ready to stagger in the direction of the Metro in his overcoat, I'll take his arm, thought Fleur, take him to my hotel, then call a medic, we have to get out of here, just then Wrath grabbed Fleur's head, immobilizing him, as though forcing him to bear witness to the direness of it all, nothing to be afraid of, Fleur, nothing really, perhaps I can't help but go back to that station at dawn every day, The Statue of Secrets, that crow of a woman waits there each day, piercing me with those eyes of hers as though I'm the prey, never speaking but seeming to say, you think I don't know who you are Wrath, but I know all, and one day you'll be mine, the trap-door to hell will open wide under your feet, then you'll be lost, perhaps, perhaps she says this, or not, this statue immobile and inaudible, but she haunts my nights out here on the cold, wet ground with the lice-ridden, a memory I once found so charming was Tai and me boating on a canal in Amsterdam, he enjoyed himself like a child, though he still sneered at me in contempt, the drawn-out cry to an impassible, indifferent world where a man's death-scream is as nothing, yet I'll forever hear it in all its tormenting slowness, even in stations at dawn, I hear it in the piercing noise of trains leaving, and still she stares at me, the Old Crow-woman, indignant or perhaps just indigent like the rest, society's reject, though·She stares down on me out of her implacable darkness, and I know that She, like so many women, carries a secret, I used to hear their confessions, you know, beautiful women admitting they no longer loved their husbands, though I reproached them from behind the grill, I had compassion for their infidelities and disobedience, not really compassion or pity, just the sovereign pride of father confessors, delighting in the discovery of sensations, a presumptuous judge listening to their intimate and contrite avowals, sniffing their perfume as they whispered to me, I can say this to no one but you and you alone, I have no carnal knowledge of my husband any more, I was raped at thirteen, and I hastened to say, was it your father or uncle, tell me humble penitent, I am listening, but they kept that secret, adding no detail, at thirteen, I asked, who could it be, as though each one had taken it all back, her tortured admission, each penitent became silent, and confession was over, then I heard them flee, I must have known how much their secret was my own, even as I despised them for confessing, their lives burned up in the first rape, once beautiful, already faded, diminished by refusal, denying men their share of pleasure, mothers despite their will, and now bringing up their own children with rigour, twelve or thirteen and ready for rape themselves, could they possibly have known how close I was to them, indissociable now that the unsayable was said, they and their children innocent and me the criminal, yes, the very man they had fled at thirteen, and whom they now turned to in adulthood with such unbelievable trust, ready as ever to dispossess them again and again in my brutal execution, the same brutality that had horrified them in youth, I had attained the summit of power that devoured my soul, the omnipotence of the rapist, you cannot possibly understand what it means Fleur, nor what it means when one loses the ecstasy of that power, to be nothing more than just another lost wanderer, despicable and living on the charity of others, when only yesterday it was I who reigned crushingly over them all, oh yes, men, women and children, the silent despot, you haven't noticed, have you Fleur, how much the very worst of tyrants, even the most barbarous dictators, love little children, Stalin bending to receive flowers from a child, such humility, such courtesy, bowing down to the ground, masters of purges and gulags seeming suddenly to crawl before little boys and girls with bouquets in a burst of purity, remembering their devoted mothers, the orthodox seminary they were sent to for piety and goodness, masters of terror incapable of an instant's reflection on the vain illusion that pulled the purity of uncouth childhood into it or the future of these adorable faces already incorporated in their calculations, faces and blonde heads offered for kisses and caresses amid the flowers, oh what sweet little things they are, tomorrow, when they are just a bit older, the Great Butcher will scatter them in tiny morsels and open his gulags and torture factories to them and their parents, beloved children executed, shot in their thousands or held in Siberian camps, the masters of terror making nice to those faces, heads, large feet, thickly matted moustaches seeming to say, may God keep you all, with all the false friendliness of executioners sharpening their knives, for they too were once such pretty young things, oh so much to regret, blood hemorraging in the country they possess and rule as tyrants, yes regret, but so it is when one is grown to manhood, a devoted mother long forgotten with the seminary, renounced and awaiting the raping gaze, devoured by those reaching down to them in drooling concupiscence, bowing obeisance made to what will soon be destroyed, innocence consecrated and bloodied already between the fingers clutching at petals, sudden applause in the Vienna concert-hall, yes, I heard them, or was it just prolonged silence, Fleur said, the contralto woman's voice with the choir, inflexions both begging and grave, I remember her words, Doctor, Doctor Death, can't your plans wait just a bit longer, you see, today all the schoolgirls of Hiroshima are outside, all of them, the air around them burns their eyelids in an instant, please Doctor Death, wait a little while longer, the orange glow will blind them forever, such a long silence, said Fleur, that I might have had time to escape, yes, get away from there, he said, and leave the rest of the band behind, but like the children in the orange glow, I stood there petrified by silence and nothingness, orange light sealing my eyes, but Wrath, still holding his arm and not listening at all, went raging on with his story, and the Other, demonic demiurge how could such mediocrity yield so many murders, he too was surrounded by young girls and boys at the ceremonial offering of flowers, oh yes, delighted and barely showing the ghost of a smile since birth, an Old Ogre, wrinkled and breathless, a quavering voice from the tomb, and bowing to one of these young flower-bearers, almost audibly murmuring behind the carnations, those who love me die with me and for me, just like my mistress and my dog, and you little one whose hair I stroke today, angels I will mold to my ethnic hatred and spite, the worst abominations, are you ready to die for me tonight, he embraced his young Aryans, this Master of racial purity and rejoiced that a brilliant architect had designed for him — ah what revenge for all his failures and rejection by the Academy of Fine Art in the days when he had only menial jobs, treated like a peasant son, now he'd show them who he was, the brilliant architect of camps in the forest where once birds had sung, deer and does ran, and barbed-wire parks for the millions of children separated from their mothers and later to be gassed as well, piled into the ovens, thus ran the thoughts of worn and shrivelled men as he leaned toward them and their flowered offerings, you my loving angels, you will all die for me, and so will your teacher, as surely as my own dog, this park is the playground of death, yes my little ones with skin so soft and hair so silken to my touch, admiring and devoted, such sweet dear little ones, your beauty surrounds me, said the manipulating Old Ogre before pulverizing them, oh they loved innocence, all of them, said Wrath, and while Su tried to sneak away to his musicians in the Metro, Wrath approached and captured him in an prolonged but open embrace, saying, it's early, and yes, I know what Tokyo would means to you, a return to health and the past when you still had all your teeth, Su, you were a child in fine form, a marvel and a musician of miracles as soon as you started playing in the streets, long before leaving for America, with its New York nights and clubs, coke and speed that ruined your body and soul, before that, with your mother and sisters, your smile wasn't twisted, but genuinely happy, oh I understand you my dear Su, you were once a healthy man, pity, Wrath said, really too bad. Running slowly now and often overtaken by other joggers, Petites Cendres thought back to the gang of youths that Yinn had gathered round him, Yinn in his conservative boy outfit, as they all were, that day — Robbie, Geisha, Cobra, Vanquished Heart, Herman, Jason (Yinn's husband), the slow-moving line filing toward the wharves in near-stupor, Petites Cendres saw them dream-like, proceeding toward the sea where the ashes of Fatalité would be interred amid roses and orchids, such harmony, so concentrated and pensive, a portrait in black-and-white as he saw it, not in the splash of variegated colours they really wore, suddenly all the pants were black, all the shirts white, all the faces an evanescent white too, murmuring, never seen to pray before but funereal now, and when he asked where they were going, they did not answer but kept on walking, unseeing, then Petites Cendres cried out to them all, Robbie, don't you recognize me, Jason, Yinn, it's me, and at that name he awoke with beating heart, for he feared Yinn's response that, in the dream, they were all soberly dressed, serious and pained on their way to the sea, and it was here Petites Cendres awaited them among orchids and roses, not Fatalité at all, but he himself, so many friends that soon the street would be crowded, oh but it was only a dream while he continued running, overtaken by the kids, sweaty in their short shorts or swimsuits, pinned by headphones and ahead of him now, they passed so close he could feel the movement of their elbows like a rocking wave, such vigorous youth bursting with health, he thought, even the not-so-young were stronger than him, but none could know his piercing desire, his fever-pitch love, whether one loves well or aimlessly, the overpowering vertigo, senseless as it all was, not the passion one endured like a brasier aflame only to be followed by searing cold, not the heat of love which loomed like an invincible mountain of ice, no matter what he felt, Robbie had said it was crucial to love and love always, at any price, for without it the muscles of the heart would atrophy, what then did Petites Cendres have to complain about, Yinn was there, constant, sometimes close by, sometimes not, but forever vigilant, and those who long to be loved, Robbie said, needed to be absent from time to time, that was a law, he said, all-knowing it seemed to Petites Cendres, his head tilted to the sky, and what else was it Robbie said, that Petites Cendres was blessed to love someone so handsome and so mysteriously divine on the stage, and what happens up there might cause less suffering than what happens elsewhere, look reality in the face, said Robbie, Yinn is not as good-looking in the everyday as you seem to think, it's his oriental mystery you're so taken with, and that's his special secret, right, trust Robbie to come up with definitions like that, he does know everything, thought Petites Cendres, but he was wrong about this, Yinn was every bit as handsome in real life as on the stage, his mystery just as bewitching, endearing and indefinable in either place, he thought, loping along slowly, deliberately, as though lulled by his thoughts, seeing the face of Yinn tilted back when he danced at the Cabaret in the midnight glow of Jason's lighting, mauve-tinted with the superimposed image of My Captain, tousled hair beneath his sailor's hat, the bold Captain who taught Yinn to scuba dive, who strolled on the deck at sunset, tender, too tender toward Yinn, so it moved Jason to jealousy, though he was too much in love with Yinn to get angry, thinking it best to remain silent and leave Yinn to his whims and fantasies till he tired of them and became faithful again as only he knew how, they were still too young, all of them, Jason thought, to wall themselves up in conjugal bonds, though he cherished the solid foundation of the marriage enough to remain faithful himself, as faithful as he'd been to his wife and was still to his children, his daughters, unshakeably, ever their protector, and also to Yinn's mother, though she remained hostile — a woman's whimsy, he thought — and Yinn was moved by this emotional stability, even as his life revolved around My Captain, and vice-versa, Robbie must be quite a snoop if he knew every little detail of their lives, and Petites Cendres couldn't stand the thought of Robbie being so close to them and aware of every part of their voluptuous relation, wholly free and happy, Robbie with them for Sunday dinner at the Captain's, champagne tastings, sent from the bed in which he entertained his friends in a pink bathrobe, surrounded by his dogs and silk pillows, and serving everyone bubbly with strawberry-and-mango fruit-cups, there were also cookies that Petites Cendres later learned were laced with cocaine, delicious they were, and Yinn couldn't wait to taste them, and when the Captain yelled, okay everyone, time for dessert, mmm, but first give me a kiss, a polite one that Yinn gave on his cheek so he could fulfill his longing, Robbie thought it was so amusing, but Petites Cendres thought it secretive and guilty; now as he ran, his feet were burning inside his sandals, and he thought of Timo, or at least his ghost, wondering if he'd made it to Mexico after being chased all the way to the border, police and guards were beating the bush for him all around, Timo the timid survivor, maybe disfigured after being slammed against a car or a concrete wall, or perhaps drowned in a swamp full of poisonous snakes, they'd been hunting cobras lately since he fled, if he'd escaped the raid his friends were caught in after selling cookies and cakes loaded with crack for a pile of money, carefully wrapped packages of cocaine too, when the sheriff burst into the apartment, it was raid-time, they had to be well organized to catch the sneaky thieves and dealers, friends of Timo, delinquents with no place safe, though he himself was a ghost in his leather vest and jewelled necklaces, maybe he'd been beaten up and killed, or maybe he survived, thought Petites Cendres, then his thoughts went to the faces of My Captain and Yinn united in a kiss, yet so chaste, so modest, as Robbie said, and he ought to know, he always did, Petites Cendres held it against Yinn as a serious betrayal, then the unconscious face of Timo superimposed itself again, whether ghost or living mortal, he couldn't tell, but either way, he was sure he'd never see his friend again, the sadness of it overwhelmed him again, if he's killed, let it be quick, so Timo couldn't dwell on his injuries, so . . . in the numbness of his run, and Daniel was still haunted by Eli the fraud and Stephen's lonely writing in Charles and Frédéric's former house, Eli would wander in at dawn from the clubs after a night of dancing with others, not Stephen, who was so alone that Daniel made an effort to visit and comfort him in a situation that worsened with Eli's hardening cruelty and addiction, yet still, to hear Stephen tell it, Eli could suddenly become exalted and put on the face of love, but not for long before falling into coldness again, this took Stephen off-guard, not knowing how to react, well, throw him out, Daniel said, you're far too indulgent with him, you'll never write your book like this, but Stephen wouldn't listen to anything so stern and sidestepped the conversation by showing Daniel an ink portrait Frédéric had drawn of Charles a long time ago, a fine depiction of the young poet and writer at twenty, on which Frédéric had written a few words in his illegible hand, to my beloved Charles, or was it the beginning of a poem inspired by others before it, my beloved Charles, the day will come when all around us is green, one day, us and us alone, flesh and bone melded together, vanished among the grasses, one day, Stephen was touched by it and would contemplate it at any hour of the night or day, you see, he told Daniel, they had an ideal relationship, absolute, nothing I will ever have with a man, certainly not Eli, I know that, and yet it's what

I crave most in life, more than the success of my books, believe me Daniel, that's really what I want, nothing more, Stephen said this as he stuffed his hash-pipe, then breathed in the fumes and coughed, Daniel took the same gently paternal tone with him as with Samuel, Augustino, and even Mai, but don't you see, Stephen, that this kid is leading you astray, why won't you understand the danger Eli poses for you? It was Stephen's candid response that surprized him, you know, Daniel, perhaps the writer in me needs to run toward danger, I can't seem to resist, weren't you like that yourself once, easily tempted, didn't you tell me you went into detox several times before you were married, d-didn't you, he stammered, hallucinate standing out on a rock by the sea, hallucinate that you saw your Great Uncle Samuel and some other rabbis shot down in the snow by German officers, and haven't you, like me, accepted being a visionary, fully knowing it could be fatal? Utterly disarmed by this, Daniel fell silent, confronted by Stephen, who had apparently smoked himself into a delirium with too much hash, and it now seemed that the one who turned a piercing gaze on Daniel was not Stephen at all, but the Charles, the Charles of Frédéric's finely drawn portrait, and it seemed to say with tempered wisdom and the sparkle of great intelligence in its eyes, Daniel, sometimes there is simply nothing we can do but wait, that's right my friend, wait till this period of craziness has passed, then will come calm and with it happiness, I wonder, will you, like me, have to leave this earth before you fully realize it? With all that, I'd still love to be at home with Frédéric, as we used to be. Could it be that Charles's youthful gaze was only for the ardours and pleasures of the young, admitting nothing to anyone, no doubt as discreet in death as he'd been in life, as Daniel thought, mute and close about his early life, it was Frédéric who had charged the drawing with such sensuality, yes, that was where it came from. And Lucia concluded at the fall of day that Brilliant was gathering up passengers with his rickshaw-bike before his evening shift at the Café Espanol, so she wouldn't be seeing him until after his night-ramblings through the taverns and bars where he recited his oral novel to anyone who would listen, sure they would weary of it, but not being written down, it constantly acquired fresh details and ornaments, as though the erudite words with which he sculpted it arose to accompany his theatrical moves and bursts of laughter, even when the story was sad, suddenly saying, you know, it was funny, real funny, they looked everywhere for three days, and all the time I was fast asleep on the train, right there with the animals in the straw, oh I had no idea how much of a beating I'd get from my black nanny, no way, I covered a lot of countryside for someone so young, and my mother the Mayoress would really let loose on me, now that was funny, a real gas, he pedalled along, Misha sitting up front beside him, okay, you don't have to bark at every red light, you know, keep quiet, it's not nice, but Misha also barked every time he heard a church bell, the shriek of a siren or the cries of a child, barking was his joy and satisfaction, so he was at it constantly, and when Brilliant said again, be quiet, Misha, can't you see we've got a pair of lovers in the back, see, they're kissing, and they need peace and quiet, you really don't get it, so just cut it out, okay, and Lucia loved the thought of those barks of recognition and gratitude when finally he returned to his life after all those misfortunes, Lucia would have loved to have a singing voice, shortly she'd put on a red shirt bought at the

Army of the Poor with coveralls over it to go cycling, the Army of the Poor, why such a short time ago she'd had her own store and a collection of dresses and shoes that made her attractive, especially to men, well that was over and done with, she reflected, Mabel had promised her a red-tailed parakeet that would never leave her shoulder, her greedy sisters had sold the store, stolen it in fact, and they were robbing her still, no more hair styling hair either, just cut it short, never to be the way it once was, long and well kept, this stripping away of everything was actually nice though, yes, she'd get used to it, she believed, at least her sisters hadn't managed to have her locked away in an institution, nor her son, ah such pathetic creatures, what would she do without Bryan here in this paradise at The Acacia Gardens, not a doubt in the world with Angel, his mother Lina and doctors like Dieudonné and Lorraine, and although she wasn't feeling pain anywhere, they simply asked her to remember, but I don't, nothing, except that I can never find my keys, and my umbrella, I lost that along with a lot of things, ah there, Bryan said the red-tailed parakeet would always be on my shoulder, I'd have a cage for night-time of course, now I mustn't forget his name, with this simple haircut, I feel like an old young man ready for any adventure, like Bryan, still such a young man himself, my son or my friend, whichever way he wants it, my sisters threw out all the empty wine bottles in the yard as if to shame me, and Doctor Dieudonné says I should cut back on the red wine, a little bit less of it each evening if I want to remember and not lose my keys or my umbrella, especially since it rains so much and I used to sleep out on the patio on cool nights, well that was because of those nasty sisters who locked me out and wouldn't let me come in, yes really, I wasn't so unhappy once I got my pets back, they licked my face and they understood me at least, better not forget to feed them, though I forget where I put their food, which cupboard, my mother would appear suddenly in the night and tell me which way was home, see, just follow me, daughter dear, like a child holding onto her dress, I followed her home, so warm and welcoming then, and I'd say to her, now tell me again Mama, it really is our house and my sisters aren't there any more, and she'd say, don't you worry so much, you're with me now, and it's your house, but you've got to remember the way, remember, and then all of a sudden my beloved mama was no longer there, and I'd fall asleep among the heavy leaves of the giant palm tree in the overgrown garden saying to myself, it's hopeless, you're going to die little by little of cold and hunger, but I'm not going to sleep outside ever again, oh if I had a bit of a voice I'd sing, I would, but at least I'll teach my parakeet to whistle, because I do sing so badly, just a thin scratchy voice, and we'd never be apart my parakeet and me, I think I've got a name for him, now I mustn't forget it the way I forget other things, Doctor Dieudonné says I have to make a list of what happens during the day, and that'll re-train my memory, he says everything has to go on the list, he says my memory isn't gone, no one's ever is, everything's always there, it's just that memory decides to wander off somewhere by itself, like me, alone and without a guide, Doctor Dieudonné says a memory that's done so much wandering has to be brought back home and taught to remember again, on the list in my notebook, I've already written that Angel smiled this morning, and Misha barked the whole way, and my parakeet's going to be called Night Out, it's on the list already, I've also written, remember to persevere, and only the present is meant to be lived in, remember now Lucia, Night Out, Night Out, my grey-and-red parakeet, yes, he's red under his wingtips, Night Out, and if I ever forget, his musical whistling will remind me, oh as pretty as a song, yes, that's how it's going to be from now on, thought Lucia, everything written down on my list the way Bryan says, him who remembers everything, I'll never forget anything, not oner thing, she thought, and little by little these blanks will all go away, that's it. When he visited Stephen, who was writing in silence in his library, Daniel went to meditate alone in the garden by the gate that was open as always, and that's when people from the past began appearing, right there at the entrance, one of Frédéric's friends who lived with his family, children and grandchildren, nearby, Grégoire it was, the old Haitian refugee, or one of his sons, who recalled Frédéric as though he were still here among them, reading and smoking heavily under the white acacia blooms that formed an arbour, with books and newspapers spread out on the table to be leafed through impatiently, while long nervous fingers tipped ashes onto them, yup, that's how I still see him, old Grégoire said, and all those cigarettes, Charles and Frédéric constantly quarrelled about it, Mr. Charles even said he smoked while he read in bed or in the library, said Grégoire, himself a heavy smoker, out here in the garden I'd wait for Frédéric each evening, and with respect in his voice, he'd sometimes said, he'd take me out in that old rattletrap car of his, he never liked the new ones, you know, my friend Mr. Frédéric, he was like that, only liked old cars, and off he'd take me to the dog races, oh Frédéric didn't like them, specially because it was so far out of town and he drove like a blind man, never did know where he was going, and the cops stopped us, you forgotten your papers again Mr. Frédéric, um, yes, I've forgotten them again, he lowered his head, but they let us go, they knew him alright from paying my son's fines lots of time so he could get out of jail, on our street they called him the poor man's lawyer, but we knew he was a musician, because we'd hear him playing the piano for hours every day, a painter too, we knew that, but we just called him our poor black man's lawyer, yup the cops knew him alright, but he didn't approve of dogs racing like that in the evening heat, graceful animals with hollowed flanks, noble creatures, no, he disliked all that and especially cursed the greedy owners, but he drove me and the kids anyway, out of kindness, he always guessed who was going to win and he whispered it quick in my ear, number five, and he was never wrong, oh he had a perfect nose for figures alright, and I got to bring home lots of money, though he disapproved of the races, he said it would be good for the kids' education, they had to go to the best schools and universities afterwards, I told you it's often said he was an advocate for poor blacks, and that's what he was, it wasn't cigarettes that killed him, though he overdid it like me, no, it was a broken heart that did it, Daniel seized Grégoire's dark, deeply veined hands in his own as Frédéric had often done, yes, he echoed, heart-break when Charles was gone, Frédéric had held them like this, saying, courage my friend, we'll get your son out, it's nothing serious, so have courage dear Grégoire, trust me, I'll talk to the Warden, and we'll work this out, after all, your son's only taken a watch, and he's got to go on with his education, the Warden has kids, he'll understand, as Daniel listened to this, he imagined writing it into Frédéric's book, then drawing on it for his own *Strange Years*, a story never before told by his venerable friend whose bowed silhouette was reflected in the mirror that surrounded the garden and made it seem less narrow and confined by houses, voices and cock-crows at all hours of the day or night, not to mention the hymns and jazzy prayers of a mixed choir in the Baptist church at all hours as well, hymns and prayers sometimes shouted and sung in a frantic rhythm that implored God and was exasperated at being heard so little, or so Frédéric had said as he rifled through the newspapers under his arbour in clouds of cigarette smoke, impatience in every gesture as others prayed for him to a god so cold and whose very existence or inexistence he deplored, he thought as an agitated agnostic, his impatience was metaphysical too, thought Daniel, who'd always known Frédéric to be nervous and agitated, except when he sat at the piano, then he was instantly peaceful, barely recognizable, no longer the same man, and as the fountain at the foot of the garden flowed into a pool where hummingbirds once came to drink, thought Daniel as Grégoire said again, it wasn't only the death of Charles, but after that Frédéric was often disappointed with his friendships, do you remember his friend Christophe, well, that was his Christian name, but his stage name was Désiré Lacroix, he wrote and performed the play *The Black Christ of Bahama Street*, and Désiré was truly crucified on the heroin cross, a tormented young man, as he said in his one-man show, the only black Christ crucified each and every day, and it sure didn't end with slavery or segregation, no matter his talent, his addiction truly sacrificed him a bit at a time, and Frédéric, who'd helped him so many times, supported him during detox, was let down completely when Désiré the Black Christ of Bahama Street, took a break from his cures to rob banks, nothing but bad people round him, he's in prison right now in California, and he took Mr. Frédéric for a ride, lied to him all along, sometimes he'd phone and say he was doing his play in jail in Los Angeles, yessir, he was a prison performer, and couldn't Mr. Frédéric send him a bit of money one more time so he could put it on for the others inside, Désiré was actually living his play, what he really wanted was for Frédéric to pay his bail again, yes, a real disappointment this one, a notorious charlatan Désiré-the-Black-Christ-of-Bahama-Street, but that's not what Mr. Frédéric said, oh no, in an excess of empathy, yes that's right, excess, especially when others lacked it so badly, Frédéric had more than he should, Christophe, he said, really was the Black Christ of Bahama Street, and I pray God he be pardoned for all his crimes and never get the death sentence, though he killed several men and he's been waiting on Death Row for years, Frédéric cried real tears over that, so you see, it wasn't only heartbreak over losing Charles, it was heartbreak for the world, said old Grégoire, and Daniel went off home to write, late and almost asleep on his feet, then waking at dawn with the nearly atonal voice still echoing in his dreams, his bowed silhouette in the garden mirrors, and still seeming to say, it's time to write Frédéric's book, and don't leave anything out, Daniel, lazy as you are, I'll get up the second time the mourning-dove sings, the first time was so melancholy Daniel fell back asleep, but the second, more staccato and yearning, got him up and held the promise of peaceful hours for writing in utter solitude, so complete, he thought, without Mélanie and the kids at home, empty space all around, he had a touch of vertigo like being drunk, it was then Daniel thought of Mélanie trotting round the country, consciously or not, thinking of her travelling through all the countries where women are oppressed and unjustly imprisoned, seeking justice for them, and despite herself, also seeking out her son Augustino, forever the object of her search, as if by chance she'd suddenly glimpse him in an air terminal or on a train, both of them travelling great distances, subconsciously, yes of course she believed in chance and the unbreakable bond that would somehow draw them closer to one another, she confided in Daniel that whenever she saw a curly-headed boy, she couldn't help turning round, hoping it was her son, she couldn't believe he'd e-mailed her over a year ago and then nothing, silence, even worse than that, inaccessible was Daniel's thought, he'd written his mother from a village near New Delhi, a very unhealthy neighbourhood he described as a slum where a mother whose son had been accused of brutally raping a young girl, himself young enough to be tried in juvenile court, so ashamed and dishonoured was the mother by her son's deeds that she never left the house where he'd grown up, not once, forever sitting against the wall with her face covered, his clothes still hanging from a cord on the wall near a calendar from which violent hands had torn and crumpled the date of the crime, Augustino wrote that he'd viewed this through the eyes of Mélanie, his own mother, who would surely understand the other woman's affliction and humiliation, Mama, I know what you'd feel if you saw her cover her face in shame and never to leave this filthy place where she watched him grow up, gazing at his clothes strung against the turquoise-blue wall, as well as her own, dyed purple and mixed with his, nothing to do but contemplate all she's lost, his backpack by itself on a nail in the prison wall, with your eyes, Mama, I saw that shame and despair as only you could, yes, yours, and as she read Augustino's thoughts so in tune with her own, Mélanie knew she'd find him again, consciously or not, she was somehow wending her way toward him, so Daniel thought, insane and unrealistic as it might seem, and in its very extravagance that's what it was, just like Stephen's blind hope that one day Eli would return peacefully to him for good, but when? Daniel, for his part, no longer went in search of Augustino, though he would always be ready to see him again, realizing that waiting and hoping for it was no more than a dream that meant nothing, but while writing his book, he probably thought of little else, so affected was he by the boy's absence, the loss of his presence, and he thus understood Frédéric's distress at being separated from Charles, the dismay of those empty hours that follow grieving, the voice of old Grégoire coming back to him and reminding him how Frédéric, finally alone, was haunted by that absurd loneliness, his piano fallen silent, no, said Grégoire, no more reading beneath the acacia bower, no, the blinds of the house closed henceforth, Frédéric seemed to live only at night now, lanky and lean, his head bowed, heading out to smoky night-clubs at night, perpetually dressed in white, all the clubs and dimly lit bars, listening to his black musician friends play, he smoked a lot and barely talked, listening to the group and following the rhythm with slow nods, one of his friends, Cornélius, a poor veteran of the Korean War who lived with his cats and dogs in a truck and always wore his decorated beret proudly, sang a negro spiritual, sometimes Mister Frédéric sang along with him when he knew the spiritual by heart, but I remember those voices, Cornélius and Frédéric, so sad in the night and on into dawn, almost faint from weariness, Frédéric going from one jazz club to another, Cornélius had a young niece called Venus who sometimes sang with him, though they said she was too young and it would be her undoing, her father was a pastor, a stern man, but young Venus' voice was voluptuous in the warm night air, but you know, I was thinking back to that time, and I was worried that Mister Frédéric brooding on the loneliness of not having Charles around would finish him, that's when I said, hey, how about going to the greyhound races, let's have some fun, he didn't want to go out, but he said sure, Grégoire, if that's what you'd like, let's go win lots of money for your sons' education, but I knew his heart wasn't in it, it would never be the same as when Charles was around of course, sometimes he'd sit in front of the TV at night, never moving, and he said in the small hours underneath the subtitles of some commercial or other, you could read the names of those who would be executed at dawn, or those who already had been, in total abject silence, like some secret shame at the killing of killers, and I think he was afraid he'd see Christophe or Désiré Lacroix, actor, across the screen he gaped at in dread, chain-smoking cigarettes without putting them out with his ash-stained fingers, and I said to him, you know, Christophe's killed five people in a bank, and he'll get the execution he's earned, you really shouldn't worry so much about him, Mister Frédéric, and he sobbed with his face in those large hands of his, you don't understand, Grégoire, no one deserves such a hellish fate, you just don't realize that Christophe is the Black Christ of Bahama Street, and that's why he's being crucified, lethal injection or electric chair, it makes no difference, he's being crucified in vain, but I told him he was making too much of it, he's just a murderer like any other, yes, he was getting carried away and needed to go and sleep it off, then one day he didn't leave his room or even get out of bed, even when Eduardo the gardner tried to get him up and dressed, all he said was, I want to be alone, please don't put yourselves out for me, that's such beautiful music I hear, he murmured, is it Ella Fitzgerald, no it's a woman in the choir at the Baptist church, no, Ella, he said again from his bed, and he never did get up after that, the only light in him was in his gaze, and it enveloped, devoured him, I remember, old Grégoire said, a light that swallowed you up and you'd never forget, then Mister Frédéric closed his eyes and said, if I sleep a bit, I'll see Charles coming to meet me, and as Daniel wrote in his book, or was it Frédéric's, he heard all these voices and tones joining his own, this was the uprising of writing, it seemed that writing would somehow finish up by bringing Frédéric back to life, his movements as he sat down at the piano maybe it was the colours he'd chosen for Greek paintings in an overflow of happiness at being with Charles, or when, as an impassioned young man, he'd painted Charles's portrait in the house that belonged to both of them, but Daniel wondered what dark heaviness, what lugubrious overtones prevailed when Daniel turned his attention to Christophe or Désiré Lacroix and the disappointment Grégoire said he'd caused Frédéric, Daniel had no idea what had happened to Christophe, was he at liberty or still locked up in maximum security in California, at once, a dark light seemed to emanate from him, as though the words Daniel wrote had given way to a troubled silence. Suddenly in his fog-bound tiredness, Petites Cendres saw before him against the sea and horizon two very young joggers, college girls, he thought, and they seemed ready for a break, hey come sit on the bench, your hair's plastered to your forehead, you sure are hot, come on and sit, rest with us, one of them said, Alex and I want to talk to you, it was as though Petites Cendres had finally been borne away on a wave that had been coming for a while, every man or woman who ran with him seemed to slide over him like a scalding wave, it was slightly oppressive with the sweat-smell of each and every one of them, though in his loneliness he enjoyed being surrounded by the sharp smell of underarms and breath elevated by the run, well, Dieudonné had told him it wasn't healthy to stagnate in bed, and now he heard the throbbing pulse in his temples and ears, wasn't that a sign of his resurrection, that made him think of the young ghosts who raised themselves at night in the Cemetery of Roses, friends struck down by the plague, young people with energy to burn, dead in appearance only, ready to rise up and dance the minute they were left behind and out of sight, waltzing in the clubs, that had to be it, he thought, these were just mistakes, young people wrongly sentenced and condemned too soon, avenging themselves as soon as night came by re-inhabiting their bodies electrified in sleep, unseen of course. Petites Cendres said they dragged him along with them in their velvety dance, they pretended to be gone, some mistaken decree somewhere had cut them down, and suddenly there he was, beneath the five o'clock sun facing the ocean on a bench between two girls covered in tattooed words of love under their cooling tops, we're newlyweds, Alex said, we thought you could help us, I'm Leo, the other one said, like Léonie; she's Alex for Alexandra, both of them in a rush of words above the early city sounds, you must be real thirsty, Alex said as she shared her water bottle with him, which he drank greedily, saying he was very thirsty, Léo said, say are you a guy or a girl, Petites Cendres smiled but didn't answer, pushing the hair back from his forehead, I'm not used to this much running any more, so girls, what can I do for you, do you know a florist shop where we can get flowers for our wedding-party, some bigot refused to deal with us because we weren't a proper couple, and they wouldn't even let us into the Youth Hostel because we aren't like the others and they don't want to encourage licentiousness, what licentiousness Petites Cendres asked, no, hey love isn't like that, those bigots get everything wrong, Léo said, but Petites Cendres at once asked, why aren't you in school or college like other girls your age, perhaps if people are intolerant it's because you're still both kids, they don't want to encourage the wrong kind of behaviour, okay they're bigoted, but aren't you too young to be married, thinking he himself was hardly marriageable, if in the cockeyed course of his life things had happened differently, perhaps he might have married Yinn, who now belonged to Jason, oh how many failures the thought of something as definitive as marriage had brought back to him, believe me, marriage is a mistake, really, he repeated in the face of their disappointment at his frank disavowal, this turned to bitterness, look I'm too old to help you, okay, he said, I can't help you nor anybody for that matter, he threw up his arms, well at least help us find a place to stay, Alex said, we want to start a new life here, we're carpenters, cabinet-makers, we can make doors and windows, you're forgetting, said Petites Cendres, around here those things just get blown away, right now, you're on an island of cyclones and tornadoes, he whispered, yeah but we're through with schools, they only give us a hard time, Alex said, so we left it all back there and took off with our dogs and bags in the car, do you know anyone who could put us up, Léo asked, it's kind of urgent, I'm sure you have someplace, he was getting irritated at their rushing torrent of words, both talking at once, then there was the noise and incessant ringing of their cell phones, well, it's a bit different for me, he said, I have a place but only for one, I'm a patient, you see, but a passing car drowned him out, you're what, Alex said, as you can see, I'm a lot older than you, and I, uh, have health issues, so it's near the hospital, a note of pride crept into his voice, everyone felt that way about the Acacia Gardens, he thought, there are a bunch of different gardens there, lemon-trees, orange-trees, pools for the doves and turtle-doves, ibises and even white egrets, I raise doves myself, which Mabel taught me to do, he added, then he realized they weren't listening, both of them on the phone, and he was unsettled by their good-naturedness as they unscrolled their plans for the week, our friends are saying be sure to catch the Triumph in Diversity Celebrations, all of it, the sailboat races and regattas, legendary, they say, what do you think of the philosophy that we're really all one true family, eh Petites Cendres, what do you say, we want to be in the crowd marching through town from sea on one side to sea on the other, the big Pride rainbow, what a sensation that'll be, for Alex and me to hold the banner in our hands and see rainbows everywhere, even on the umbrellas and parasols and stretching all the way from sea to sea across town, our day and our party, are you going Petites Cendres, holding the banner and all, pierced ears, too many necklaces and pendants, like the little cross-dresser Cheng up on stage for the first time, these girls may be as timid as Cheng, but they aren't both boy and girl the way he is, and they're much more outgoing, Alex said, I wrote a thesis on Separate Species, you see, all Living Species must be brought together out of respect for each of them, that's what I wrote, and my prof rejected it, end of term dissertation, Alex said, and all the others made fun of me, so that was that for my studies, at that school anyway, that's when we took off down the road, Léonie, me, the dogs and our things, so whaddya say Petites Cendres to No Separate Spaces out of respect for all living things, one big family the way it says here, hesitating, Petites Cendres said, oh one big family might be an illusion, you may not know it yet, but each of us is alone, in fact a species by itself, with its own space, when they're all mixed together in a community, doves and dogs included, you've got to remember we're animals too, the others are superior to us when they live in groups, they show more solidarity, that's right, I learned that from watching my doves, the only wars with pitiless fighting are those of men, all of a sudden, Petites Cendres felt like a preacher scolding children, he realized he'd stayed away from any new human contact for a long while, anything that could possibly upset him, it went back to when Yinn had introduced him to Cheng, the young disciple he'd trained for the stage, repelled by the presence of a second Yinn in the spotlight, though the first remained master, indulgent toward the new one, almost a father, no, Petites Cendres appreciated neither his presence nor the novelty of his style, especially sharing prominence with Yinn, it was infuriating that the latter would let himself be supplanted like this, especially by a performer barely more than a child, but the other girls annoyed him too, using Petites Cendres' despair as a distraction, just as Cheng did, then, to make himself useful and less pathetic, he remembered that Alex and Léo were wood-workers, and the gardens could use their brawn and skill to make doors and windows for the unfinished homes that were lapsing into disrepair, but first he'd have to talk to the head volunteer, which he told the girls he'd do, they hugged him with their junky cell phones dangling off them, hey, that's right, you could put us up for one night, we can see you don't like being put out, same as the injustice of Separate Species that can't get hooked up with others, well I got to keep running till sunset, right let's up and go, said Léo, we'll run with you, the dogs and bags can wait in the car, oh boy, this is going to be some celebration, we mustn't miss any of it, the regattas, the races, the huge rainbow banner for us to hold, sea to sea, just down the street from one bit of ocean to the next, yes, that's right, said Petites Cendres as though waking from his soporific dream of brilliant colours, all of us together. Daniel's book had to include his encounter with the photographer Rémi in the garden with the magnifying mirror, about Daniel's age, he'd come to do the house along with those of other artists and painters, what Daniel considered youthful maturity for a creative man, though perhaps a little self-indulgent, whereas his kids saw him as a very mature man and already short of breath, hmm, of all the painters' and artists' homes, it was Charles and Frédéric's that amazed him the most, because he always felt pacified when he entered this garden with the memory of hearing Frédéric at the piano and perhaps seeing the two silhouettes as they practised a Bach étude together, as well as an intimate conversation between Jean-Mathieu and Caroline — whom he admired discreetly — over a book they were working on together, when he met Daniel there, Rémi told him about being a war correspondent and photographer, he said wars were as common as beauty was rare, and in his early days he'd witnessed many, one after another, that marked him so badly he'd had to give it up and get away from the conflicts that tore at his conscience so much he no longer wanted to live, depressed by his powerlessness to help the dying each day on the battlefield, he had a son of twenty he was afraid would be called up to go and fight, do we really take care of our children so we can pack them off to such atrocities, that's what my wife often says, so we live in fear for our son, besides, who would want to steep his fate in unending tragedy, Rémi went on, still he was deeply sensitive and said he'd had a revelation about beauty as he went through Jean-Mathieu's books and Caroline's photos of contemporary history, he often returned to photograph the house, and always thought of them, one chronicling the life and work of other authors, the other taking their portraits, they had published several books together on the poets, authors, and artists of their time, fusing their respective arts simply and without artifice, Rémi said, resulting in such rare beauty compared with the daily exhibitions of violence around them, almost sacred amid the wars and conflicts, a beauty they'd been able to depict as deep and lasting, a triumph, in fact, over the ugliness of crime, Daniel recalled that Jean-Mathieu had long hesitated over these projects, perhaps because working together might cast a shadow on their love, Jean-Mathieu knew her and the intransigence and the harshness she brought to her work, in those moments when they ate out on the terrace as winter flowered, or leaned out toward the emerald waters of the Gulf of Mexico, it was then she recorded everything about his face, as he touched his bald head, he'd say embarrassed, you know, Caroline, I don't have much time, and I've got to finish my book, do you think your project could wait a bit, and she, feeling her own demands, said, you and only you can write about the modern poets you've known so well, tomorrow it'll be too late, they won't be modern any more, everything vanishes so quickly, you have to strike in the moment, and I'm going to need a better camera for a more filtered image, he could feel her passion and fervour, probably couldn't resist them, you know, he used to say, some are destroyed by depression, cancer or suicide, or not at all, he was disillusioned in the face of Caroline's willfulness, which to him seemed more like fierce stubbornness, women have to have it, and everyone has to leave a trail behind them, it's essential in photography, that's what Caroline would say, and as Daniel wrote, it was as though he actually heard them, but it was Rémi talking about their works that so profoundly moved him here and now in Charles and Frédéric's garden, the books, like their authors and the traces they left, as Caroline said, Rémi recalled a black-and-white portrait of Charles made when one of his first books came out, the thin smile of a stunningly precocious young writer, a book that Jean-Mathieu would later edit, in it Charles was facing away from Frédéric at the piano and sheet music, in a study hall or practice room beneath the beams of an old house, a frail young man, or rather an adolescent writer that Frédéric had always wanted to protect, even in their own home, always full of guests, Frédéric loved anything magical, Rémi said, he even had a false bookcase built over a hidden door where he disappeared into his office, sometimes for whole evenings at a time, it was a counterpoint to the magnifying mirror in the garden, a haven of silence in his writing sanctuary he could never tear himself away from to frequent other people, and in this room with Dante, said Rémi, yes long hours re-reading Dante, that's right, I remember, said Daniel, I was starting out as a writer then, got married, Mélanie and were I so deeply in love, not parents yet, and I wasn't wholly out of the woods with my drug habit, oh I loved her, but inside I was in pieces, yes, that's how it was back then, Daniel was amazed that he confided so much to Rémi, whom he'd barely met, but this observer of so many struggles and wars seemed to understand perfectly, I was definitely haunted then, but less so now, no, I think not, what haunted me was the thought that a nuclear summer would lead to our deaths in a nuclear winter or some other devastation that would leave no one to tell the tale, that is the obsession that drives all my writing, grandiose, said the photographer, and the only one that can be allowed to dominate us, because some day, even without any terrorist action, but just because we're so careless, never thinking about the proliferation of nuclear weapons, it will simply happen, said Rémi in an even, toneless voice, as though he had thought about it so much he became indifferent whenever his thoughts turned that way, so now at least it didn't hurt as much, I know that's how we'll end, he went on in the same voice, but suddenly the intensity of the subject became too painful, Rémi went back to talking about Charles and Frédéric with renewed energy, there's a commemorative plaque to Charles's work that Frédéric had put up at the entrance to the house, so his name would always be honoured for his writing, just as it was willed to become a residence for future writers, I often think when I walk by with all my cameras, and I can't seem to get it out of my mind, that I see everything as though through a lens, it must have been like that for Caroline, the outer image is fixed before entering our bloodstream, fixed in our mind's eye with all its grains and imperfections, then we work it over, till it's pristinely clear, but first it must inhabit us and stir us with its reality, be it a face or a mountain, one has to be conquered, seduced by what we see, yes, when I pass by the house, I regret not seeing Frédéric's name up there with Charles's, he always allowed Charles's reputation to eclipse him, didn't he, and Charles often reproached him for it, saying Frédéric's modesty bordered on nonchalance, even indolence, for Frédéric was the more artistically gifted of the two, embracing every medium and all of humanity, sometimes with a certain lack of discrimination, Charles noted with a hint of irony, Frédéric himself said that perhaps he was a virtuoso in all the arts, but he lacked rigour, never having spent a whole day writing his books and articles the way Charles did, oh he'd written a lot when he travelled alone, but as a psychological support, Frédéric said, like the articles on poor Mexican families so impoverished and left to themselves that they all lived together on the rails, the prey of famished dogs weak with want themselves, the number of trains and wagons got less every day, and these articles, written in haste, were meant to soothe Frédéric's conscience, whereas for Charles, writing was an ascetic discipline, oh he'd played Grieg's *Lyric Pieces* at twelve, along with Mendelssohn's *Concerto*, a born musician, said Frédéric, but, absence of rigour or not, he'd preferred a life of greater freedom than a concert pianist could enjoy, he also took care not to upset a younger brother who envied his success, no, displeasing or offending anyone repelled him deeply, what delighted him the most was painting, this could offend no one, words like these came from sheer modesty, Rémi said, feeling himself the poet Charles's guardian, protector and fortress, and so it was that he went downhill while Charles was in India for so long when Cyril came into his life and upset the peace of his writing retreat, Caroline had called him Charles's jealous demon, though she maintained we all had to meet our Devastating Angel one day or other, all the more surprising since Charles had always thought himself more cerebral than carnal, ah yes, but one day that Angel appeared and destroyed all beliefs and illusions with one stroke of his sword, every delusion we have about ourselves, Caroline said, and surely she was right, Rémi remarked, Charles was far from suspecting any such thing when he went on a retreat to write in an Indian ashram, so spiritual and ascetic was the path of illumination that led him there, even as she listen to his confidences, Caroline was totally ignorant that her own Angel was right there at the door, for Charly would be her downfall just as surely as Cyril was to be Charles's, neither of them had seen this coming, wisdom isn't necessarily born in us, said Rémi as he fiddled with his camera, Daniel watched the skilled movements of his hands as if the thought of the idea of taking Daniel's picture for his collection on writers made him more exuberant, this is what Caroline intended with her own collection of writers still alive and kicking, yesterday's Moderns having turned into mere representations, as she put it, Rémi too remembered them all after so much to-and fro across the living-room of this house of poets in his hippie boots and long hair flowing down his back, he'd been too timid to address anyone before being a reporter of wars and global conflicts, but he'd told Charles that one day he'd write, maybe even be a journalist, sure, who knows what awaited him, countrysides on fire and so very many dead, there was no knowing what lay in store, such yearning to be struck down so fast and so soon, he said, I don't want my son called up, but he's twenty and he wants to go, he says it's his mission, he'll do us all proud, see, my dear Daniel, how contrary life can be, even malevolent, when it comes to each person's desires, I can't transplant my experiences into my son, he'd never understand them anyway, faithless, that's what it is, Cyril destroying Frédéric's faith bit by bit before the coup de grace, but maybe it all started earlier with Jacques and the former sporting god's slow physical and intellectual disintegration, once strong, seemingly invincible, photographed by Caroline in his last days, shivering from cold wearing corduroy pants in summer, the picture of him was immortal though, I can still see him, his blue eyes much softened, no longer seductive, a man enamoured of conquests, not a man diminished or defeated by an illness as yet unnamed, but known to be devastating and deadly, first called Other People's Illness to avoid labelling it a skin disease, supposedly contracted only by those condemned by their behaviour or the colour of their skin, so they were different, its virulence was not yet understood, nor the extent of its reach along the shadowy paths of ignorance, then overflowing them to penetrate everybody's home, it was Jacques' photograph, almost serenely tender in all his nudity, this was the new face of tenderness he offered us, as though it were already present though unnoticed, Rémi said, a kind of gift or supernatural treasure, as if to say, I know this will hurt you, for we must part, but don't worry so, it's not that long till we meet again somewhere else, that's all, there's nothing more I can say to convey what I'm feeling, Rémi stopped, still summoned by Jacques' gaze and embarrassed by it, yes, Daniel said, it all began with

Jacques, Frédéric's decline, Charles's infidelity in the ashram, the first tear in the fabric of their strong ties and peaceful life together, yes Jacques and the shock of a scandalous death, one of the first to fall victim, so cruelly too, not even knowing what afflicted him, nor even that he was sick at all, just a few spots on his face, nothing, he laughed it off without a care, laughed like one not used to suffering, yet one of the first marked for death by this remote disease, Other People's, said Daniel to Rémi, thinking of these words full of sorrow, yes, he'd jot them down tomorrow. Beneath the bridges, Wrath still held them under his lugubrious spell, Su and Fleur both, though the latter wasn't thinking of Wrath only as a down-and-out worthy of disgust and nothing more, no, while Wrath ranted on bombastically, he thought about how he could save Su, he might carry the frail musician in his arms, he reflected, then at Fleur's hotel by the quays, he'd let him rest in the room, though coke addicts are often stronger than they look after the drug has taken its toll, Su's nerves got stronger with every injection, even if it meant perilously speeding up his heart, when we get there, Fleur said, I'll call a medic while he's napping, but will he go along, he thought he could save Su, if only for a few more hours or days, and this brought Fleur new hope, he could still rejoin the orchestra in time for their next concert in Switzerland, then two girls in scarves and winter coats showed up looking like ghosts, so pale against the glare of the street lamps, these are my young gypsies come to empty your pockets, to rob you right before my eyes, said Wrath, see how shameless and brazen they are, later they'll approach cars on the off-ramps of the highway and pretend to squeegee their mirrors and windows, oh yes, I know them alright, they're here every night before they go see their pimps in the cheap hotels, sure I know them, Wrath said, watch out for their charmed hands and fingering finesse which will latch onto anything, the ones that don't have pimps, too young maybe, sleep in vacant lots or squat in warehouses by the docks, they get chased away but always come back, their men looking out for them, brothers or uncles or fathers, selling them the way their mothers did from birth, mothers holding them in their arms to offer whenever the markets open, stretched out on blankets with their infants, sometimes two of almost the same age up against the *porte-cochères*, the stain of human misery in the middle of nice neighbourhoods, handsome monuments and beautiful church gates, oh yes, they're a stain on all of it, not for the kids to lay blame on, that's up to us, but we can't know what they're feeling, they're devoted, and communion for them is begging, medieval work in these years of progress, highly visible though, but still we don't see them, we place a coin in the baby's hand, a filthy kid, little ones in the arms of consenting mothers, and get the most ambiguous smiles of all, from a corolla of covers over both of them, cold days and colder nights, the mother says, thank-you, thank-you sir with a note of triumphalism, and God bless you, even the baby's smile is one of malignant ambiguity, holding the coin in its muddy hands, his mother figures he shouldn't be too clean for the task at hand, oh, yes, their eyes tell me what they're thinking, sure, soon we'll be hip-deep in them, he said brusquely chasing off the two girls as he had the Old Woman, his wide hand emerging out of the blackness, we'll take apart all their shelters and camps and caravans in the city-centre, who needs all that noise and filth, do you think they'll ever go back to Bulgaria, 'course not, we'll merely evict them from this budding medievality of ours, oh it's growing fast, Wrath said, they're our ultimate secret, and one day with feigned alarm and shame, we'll have to reckon up what we owe them, they are our secret and unmentionable wounds, but in the meantime, we simply clear them out, women and children in their huge, sprawling campgrounds, and out they go by the thousands, to railway lines and highway ditches, our new Middle Ages with its very own epidemics and sanitary perils, yet still they come from all over, river banks, rickety boats, indeed everywhere, said Wrath, but one of the young women spoke up angrily, shut up Old Man, you don't know what you're talking about, her eyes shone with a dark glow against her pallid face, as though she were almost frozen, her voice trembled, we have our saints to defend us, and worker-priests who fight poverty in our villages, she lectured him, you who talk such a good show, evil that you are, how can you judge our misfortune, we have our faith in God, and some mayors who are on our side buy new, clean trailers for us to move into once in a while, they aren't the ones exploiting our misery, and soon our kids will be good in school, and we've got the worker-priests on our sides too, oh yes, she said, our camps won't be so ragged any more, we'll be earth's inhabitants like everyone else, with our own homes and houses that no one can throw us out of to live in the mud, yes, God is with us, Wrath heard her out in a passive pose, then suddenly, as if forgetting how brutally he'd repulsed them only moments ago, he began to speak in a familiar tone as though to a friend, though still a bit condescending, my friends Cora and Elvira, I pass judgement on your misery because it is the same as my own, I too sleep outside in the bushes and vacant lots, I know your smell as surely as you know my own, I'm not the same as when I took the bread and pay away from others, and most of all, don't you dare mention God, it will only deepen your misfortune, like you, I am an exile, a pariah, and Elvira shot back, oh we'll get a place to live, for God is with us, and the worker-priests support us, her sister chimed in, yes, the mayor promised us a place to live, we'll be welcome in the villages, and later our kids will go to school instead of being carried away with our shacks when the rivers overflow, modular housing made of wood, Elvira cut in, look, I'm one of you, Wrath said, the old ecclesiastic with a soul every bit as ruined as his body, oh yes, I'm part of this roving circus too, this ambling through the Middle Ages with you from country to country and city to city, yes, even displaying all these shameful and secret wounds, but who sees or hears us, who sees or hears you, he told Cora, you with your dark skin, you'll see, you'll see how they separate you out, you'll still be victims, and your kids are not going to play with the other kids, nor will they eat hot meals in the school cafeterias with the white kids, segregation will split their classes in two, of course it will, and you won't get your schooling, they'll deny you and keep you mentally backward, the same as in Slovakia, believe me, that's how it's going to be, and above all don't bring God's name into it, it's another name for Hate, Wrath said, we're all of us victims of His hatred, we have our faith, said Elvira, and it's the only thing that will never betray us, Cora added, the worker-priests are with us rebuilding the lost caravans, oh charge ahead my brothers, or tomorrow our children will laugh at you all, because our hour will come indeed, Wrath replied, right Cora and Elvira, you know as well as I do that hour will come only when you've destroyed everything, our houses, our lots, everything, but he was talking to himself, the young women in their winter coats and scarves having fled up the stone steps to the street, Fleur looked up at it and thought to himself, that's the way Su and I will go, easy, I'll drag him with me, he weighs next to nothing, but he's got all his sheet-music under his arm, and he won't stop smoking, how am I going to convince him we've got to get out of here, this ice-cave in hell, Wrath cut in, as you can see, we get all kinds through here, Cora and Elvira are gone, no need for me to stop them, they'll be back first thing at dawn with their haul to fence, it won't take long for men to wear them down, that's right, I'll spot them in a station busy exercising their light fingers, I know the type, the Old Woman yelled, what about Tai, what have you done with Tai, she walked up to Wrath and grabbed him by the coat, don't you touch me, he said, even if my coat is mangy, you'll make it even filthier, what have you done with Tai, eh, where is he, and Wrath mumbled, apparently to himself, it's not my fault the boat tipped over, or that he hung out with people who could get me in trouble and thrown in prison, that's right, the boat got caught in the wind, but he was talking so low now that neither Fleur nor Su could hear him, you're on the "wanted" list shouted the Old Woman, you're the one that killed Tai, she murmured, and Wrath pushed her furiously away, you're nothing but a toothless old whore, a witch, no matter what you think, I loved Tai, his brothers and sisters too, even corrupted priests like me have spotless souls, for a long time we believed we were God's true children, the chosen ones, and what deludes us is all that madness about redemption and salvation, our purity safeguarded by possessive mothers, all ready for the priesthood, well the purity is deviant, repugnant and knowingly cultivated by the presumptuous secrets that our mothers purchased with their "Hail Marys", then sold us like peddlers of children's souls, sold us to God, nothing we can do or say, like child slaves in the marketplace, also sold by mothers to cities with the State's silent consent, not wanting to acknowledge the dirty little secrets everyone knows, in streets, that's right, on the porches of houses, churches and museums, mothers peddling their children in public, right next to the kindergartens where the middle-class kids play, where their nannies knit woollen outfits so they won't catch cold, nobody hears the coughing baby held by its mother on the sidewalk, because they're pariahs, only steps away, filthy beggars sitting on the asphalt, you know, Old Woman, if they look for me here, they'll never find me around you, because they're looking for you too, thief, lying spiritist, and no matter what you may think, I saved Thai and his family from the grotesque misery of an orphanage and prostitution, sure, you'll say it was that madness for redemption and salvation that caused my downfall, and you'd be right, I was brought up in guilty virtue, dreaming of pomp, and I fell for the siren-call of privilege like so many others, parading in gilt robes like some giant doll, a princess of devotion, while they feminized me with lace and embroidered chasubles. Hooded robes studded with pearls, I was so drunk on my vanity, chaste perhaps but powerful, such a dishonest and circumscribed chastity, I gloried in it, chastely approaching the orphanages to save their bodies, each little one enclosed with me in abstinent love and under tight control, nothing dawned on me, suffering in symbolic castration beneath the luxury of my robes, outraged and, yes, modestly holding in an immense desire for caresses, for a man can dominate a child, but never the reverse, be it Tai or anyone else, I'll always feel myself chastely pulling away from license without fully realizing it, that's the way of it, I bought a child's body out of its ugly misery, I felt neither sensual nor sexual about it, I simply knew I had to have it, usurp it, everything was mine by right and without distinction, no matter what, thus was my inherent power, my royal right, like that of centuries past, and thus I must act and in no other way, led astray by the hypocrisy of a pure soul, and be it Tai or another, I was in the habit of possessing whatever had no strength to resist me, thus was I a man debauched and dissolute, one whipped on by a passion for virtue, rather the latter, for what is more virtuous than a young child, and I was in the throes of rapacious purity, disturbing and treacherous, wanting to save what came toward me in utter candour, but such chastity and abstinence are a perilous hatchery to crime, what could you possibly know, Old Woman, of a virtuous soul lending itself to every kind of poison and believing above all else in its own domination, its duty to rescue, Wrath said while she continued to howl in the motionless air of this spring evening, Wrath, what have you done with Tai? Lucia's forehead beneath her short hair had a look of insolence, and she wore blue coveralls, now she stopped her bike on the path by the sea because her parakeet Night Out had reminded her with a soft whistle that it was snack-time as he clung to the handlebars and balanced himself with his claws, oh I've got your corn cookies, Lucia said to the bundle of grey and red feathers as she opened her backpack, and I've got a bunch of grapes, and you can have some of those too, Night Out, Night Out, she repeated as she faced the reddening sky, the sea was still calm, the beach and bathers were cooling as the evening breeze moved in with the pink-and-red light, soon the sun would set, a veritable blaze among the clouds, she said to the bird whose curved beak devoured the cookie crumbs, occasionally lifting its round head for a snatch of song, a melodious but high-pitched whistle, Lucia thought, and she said out loud, how well Mabel taught you to sing, oh we're soon going to be inseparable, you and I, Lucia thought too of Brilliant soon bringing supplies to the residents of The Acacia Gardens with his usual, quick hippity-hopping gait, well the special residents anyway, and by that he meant the ones who didn't get out much any more, there were special vitamin-enriched meals for them, personal delivery straight to your rooms, he called it, got 'em from the Café Espanol where I work, so I know they're delicious, 'cause I want to make sure you have an appetite, and even the ones who really didn't feel up to eating seemed to be lifted by his appearance with the delicious-smelling boxes, when it came time for breakfast and supper, right for each one, he was funny too, thought Lucia, oh yes, she was lucky not to be one of the sick ones who rarely got out, she had her health and a lovely sunny place to live, and to top it off, Mabel had given her the most affectionate of her parakeets, so she really had no need to feel sorry for herself as a woman alone, as long as she had Night Out to keep her company, and of course Brilliant, all these new friends here at the gardens, too, not to mention personal physicians, Drs. Dieudonné and Lorraine, in case she had a memory lapse and forgot her keys or her umbrella, one of those blanks that happened when she might forget who she was or stayed fixated on a particular word or thought, some idea that suddenly somehow didn't fit, it must be all that red wine she'd been drinking these past years, that can't be good for her, that's what Dr. Dieudonné said, no, that was no way to escape life's little worries, he'd say, still, she thought, her sisters hadn't managed to strip away every last bit of her dignity, and if she hadn't run into Brilliant one drunken night, today, she might this very minute be thrown in with a bunch of handicapped and elderly people in some home, she felt so young, how could she even imagine such a thing, her sisters would surely have abandoned her over a few memory blanks, or maybe got rid of her because of the occasional spell of dizziness or panic when she was in her cups, she wondered how she'd deal with eternity or the end of it all, she had no stomach for either one, for both seemed so boring, like waiting for the dentist, she hadn't the faith for either one, she'd asked Mabel about it, she had enough faith for any two people, so she wasn't the least bit worried, nope, she'd pray the Lord, she was always in church anyway, but there were some things she couldn't forgive, like Merlin her innocent parrot being killed by some criminal kid, no, even the Lord couldn't let that one slide, and she'd get even with him for sure, she fiercely swore an oath on it, how she'd do it wasn't quite clear yet, she knew the Lord wouldn't be happy about it, but that's the way it was going to be, and when it came to Merlin's spirit, she figured the soul of a parrot had to live eternally in a lush green paradise specially for parrots to rest in, sure, that had to be it, but I'm just a poor old black woman selling ginger drinks, what do I know about all this stuff, Lucia, how could I, eh, I don't know everything about religions, all of them, like Reverend Ezéchielle, she went on admiringly, but she did say in her sermon that whoever killed Merlin would be punished, he'd go to jail, she knows about every religion and that's a whole lot, let me tell you, Mabel said to Lucia, still she always says that despite the variety of them, there's only one true doctrine, and that's Ezéchielle's, so simple you wouldn't believe it, love one another, that's all, oh but it doesn't include whoever killed my parrot, oh no, and Lucia listened to Mabel go on about the lush green parrot paradise and palm-lined avenues and green pastures, maybe a few white sheep here and there, but still, when the panic attacks started about her future on earth or wherever else it might be, the definition of Mabel's parrot-paradise was not much comfort, a ball of abstraction as threatening as any number of asteroids, and much closer, seemed almost to brush the earth in its path across the universe, so that one day she'd be swallowed up in it, so thought Lucia, who for so long lived a proper and acceptable lifestyle, though maybe all lives were like that, sure there was inequality between the sexes, and one had to live within those confines, no choice, she thought, no, she'd had her childhood with those sisters, then marriage and the birth of her son, divorce, oh so many regulation steps to go through, one norm after another, and they were always hers, next came what is called a woman's fallow period after child-bearing, another phase of inferiority to submit to, that was when she chipped away at the mould a little, but so little, she had her store, her jewelry, a career of her own, loves of her own choosing, the so-called sterile season of life had been fruitful for her, abundant and never boring, then all of a sudden she had to get back in line for what they called old age, that too had been foreseen, and though she wasn't ready for it yet, her greedy sisters had prodded her toward it despite her wishes, she was having too much fun with all the young people she hung out with in bars and who brought her home, Lucia was still kicking over the traces a bit, she was getting to be troublesome, but she was rich, so perhaps it was necessary to convince her she was unhinged, especially with all those animals and her other eccentricities, perhaps she should be placed somewhere, after all her memory was a bit faulty, people like that really shouldn't be out and about, they needed caring for, a place to rest, that's what her sisters said, and she'd heard all these hostile murmurings and they worried her, it was true she'd gone blank once in a while lately, when she tried to recall a face or a phrase, and they multiplied in her head, what with these headaches and all, nothing too precise though, but it was certainly no howling chaos either, when Brilliant spoke softly to her, she grasped every single word, and it was so pleasant to hear him laugh, and she spontaneously laughed with him, even about her blanks, then forget about them, here have some more red wine, Brilliant would say, it's the wine of happiness, it's our celebration of friendship, Lucia thought to herself, at last I have a friend who's sincere, and Brilliant is his name, that was the whole story as she told it to Night Out, the pretty bird who'd left cookie crumbs on her coveralls and in her hair when he flew from the handlebars to her shoulder, the soft down of underfeathers against her cheek. On his deck chair by the sea, cherry cocktail in hand, Adrien was thinking about his cleaning-lady Dorothea, so dedicated to maintaining the crease in his white trousers with daily ironing, sad that she'd been illiterate for such a long time, but now he was teaching her to write, and she certainly had earned the attention of a scholarly man with plenty of free evenings to help her learn, Suzanne in her altruism would certainly have approved, though it was not his prime quality, he reflected, in fact he'd alluded to it in his poem "Giving Account", to be altruistic one had to love one's fellow man, and he rarely reached the level of tepid tolerance, often finding even that a stretch, it was barely two hours since Daniel had parted company with him, but why, since he was about to say in all good will that *Strange Years* was much more a chronicle of his children's times than his own, in the way of raucous rock, do you know that punk groups sometimes play in churches, sacrilege I say, and that's how I see your style and thinking, he was going to say, or maybe he had already, and that's when Daniel made his escape, yes, interspersed screaming and gospel song, that's what it is, Adrien said, that's your book for you, believe me, I'm not a pious man, but that sort of no-class music in a church, well, there's just no beauty in it, rather a kind of black mass, I'd say, but Adrien had misspoken, and Daniel would hear no more, well, it was still a shame he'd left so abruptly before Adrien had a chance to explain his theory on Daniel's *Strange Years*, all in needless detail and decoration for which an agitated contemporary public would have no patience, what he had forgotten to say was that in our world of renewable excitement, you must admit my dear fellow, nobody reads us any more, I taught young girls for a good many years, and if anyone still reads me it's because my thinking is primarily theoretical, my wife was the lyric one, and that is why her poems are so touching, personally I've always avoided the emotions, though I must admit that in my latest poem "Giving Account", and I'm constantly reworking it, the extremes of emotion cause me discomfort, well, even if Daniel was a barbarous writer, thought Adrien, they could still have exchanged a few intelligent ideas, but no, he'd simply turned his back and fled, and Adrien was left between sea and sky smarting under the insult, possibly Adrien himself was to blame for having hurt this sensitive writer however inadvertently, still Daniel was Isaac's nephew, and that made them distant relations just the same, Adrien wished he'd mentioned his son Georges's offer to have him move in with the absent-minded mathematics teacher, his wife and the grandkids, but he turned it down, not wanting a crowd in his life, especially children, ah for the solitude and sanity of a poet blessed by the gods, such was his thought, besides I can't bring myself to leave the house where I so loved your mother, he wrote on his tiny portable computer then stretching out in his deck chair, comfortable in his certitude, and tonight he'd dine with Charly, and that would crown his day of sun and waves warmed by the winter mists, so, that's it, I'll live alone with my fine Dorothea every day when she's not in church, and that's that, she's a fine student who wants nothing more than to read and write, although alas, it will mostly be for Bible reading and hymn singing, even if my left ear's very weak, I'll still hear them only too well, pity I can't interest her in something else instead, Adrien had written to his son Georges as well, dear son, I may be naïve, but I do sense the presence of your mother nearby, really, it's as though she's mysteriously writing away behind the screen, do you remember it, Georges, with the white lotus on it, yes, indeed, I'm afraid Suzanne, mother to all of you, did have some woolly-headed and exotic beliefs, I really do regret that her faith in some imaginary nirvana keeps her at a distance and always will, as he typed out his piece on the keyboard, he heard her last words: *Daleth*, there is a door that opens onto a luminous sea, when it is open, there will be nothing to fear for anyone ever, she said to him, though he was increasingly deaf, he heard her clearly with his left ear, a refrain of shattering sonic density. The house was deserted and childless, Daniel was still frequently disturbed while writing, there had been the crushed lizard, the night silence, and at dawn when he got up to see the mauve rays of the sky at dawn out on the patio, then of course the alarming calls from Stephen which had whittled away at his silence like a mouse in the walls of a country house nibbling on the haughty silence of the woods, for this was all he heard, then Stephen phoned, asking urgently if he could come right away, I have to speak to you in confidence about Eli, these moments by the pool when Stephen complained about all the insects in the garden and lizards in the grass, I also spotted some snails in between the wooden laths, and the pool is as tiny as a bathtub, how did such people as your distinguished friends manage to live in such primitive conditions this way and with no air-conditioning in their rooms, ah at last it was out there, he'd held it in for so long and now out it slipped, for a policeman had knocked at the door that morning and asked if Eli lived there, Stephen said no, he was neither an informant nor remotely disloyal, he told the intruding cop he didn't know Eli, I see, well we have an arrest warrant for him, with a shrug he politely excused himself for bothering Stephen, who was in his bathrobe, and as he listened, Daniel ruminated on the large number of arrests that had taken place in this house when Frédéric was still trying to rehabilitate Désiré Lacroix, his Black Christ of Bahama Street, along with a string of delinquents whose bail Frédéric had paid, so they wouldn't have to spend months or years in jail, platoons of bad boys, according to Rémi, that the dandy

Stephen knew nothing about, in fact, he hadn't done much living at all, Daniel reflected, and maybe that was the root of his bitterness at the downfall with Eli, but Daniel brought himself up short at this sketchy judgement of the younger man, after all, how can you blame a young person for his lack of experience, again he was conscious of having been too ready to judge what he did not know in his own son Samuel, well, I told him to shove off, Stephen related, just the way you suggested, but boy did he react violently, I'll leave when I damn well want to, he yelled, and I had the urge to throw all his stuff out into the street, the evening-wear for night clubs, the obscene swimsuits, and suddenly I realized everything about him was annoying and repelling, really repulsive, and it was my fault for letting him into Charles and Frédéric's house and allowing him to run downhill, shameful, what a rotten choice I made, Stephen said, when all I really wanted was a loving companion, just that, Charles and Frédéric were like that for one another all their lives, loving companions, he said as the outpouring of nostalgia died away, he couldn't believe he'd be alone forever, and as Daniel listened to this monologue, his mind drifted back to Rémi with all his cameras strung around his neck, saying, I don't want my son to see what I have seen, all these heroic women in war, alone at the scene of disaster while the suicide truck just keeps burning and the tires explode in a plume of fire and smoke, stoic figures, each woman alone covering her face and her tunic the colour of the fire, crying in Somalia near the empty presidential palace, and behind her a militant or daughter or mother of the kamikaze at the wheel, the woman a lone survivor out of ten, all dead, no, my son mustn't see what I've seen, but there's worse still, he told Daniel, and that's what you fear for your own kids, as you said, it's as though we re-play the newspaper photo of a young man with a very harsh face, beneath a crisp cap as he waits for the missile to launch, the exterminating soldier, deadly serious, defiant above and beyond the stony hardness of a silent spirit, deaf to reason and to the world, and what does that face really show but servility, the servility of a guard obedient to its master or prince in frenzied madness, the madness of having tasted the total devastation of others by this wayward master, the extreme servility of a guard or a soldier exploited, like the rocket Unha 3, such a harmless-sounding name, whether launched in North Korea or elsewhere, and so we no longer see our children, nor they us, said Rémi, oh I'm no pessimist, he went on, it's the way things are, I'm not afraid of the dark, like soldiers who can see the enemy coming, even at night, but I do need to know who it is and if they're coming with guns, bombs or rockets, especially the Unha 3, that's the one they don't talk enough about, they keep it hidden, then let loose at a moment's notice in an act of furious obedience to their master . . . Stephen suddenly shouted, you're not listening, are you, you're lost in thought Daniel, about what, gee I'm sorry I bore you so much with Eli's probably getting locked up, yes, I know he'll get caught when he's prowling around the discos at night, and he didn't come home last night, then, you'll see, I'll get the news he's been thrown in jail, though I'm not the one who blew the whistle on him, but it's bound to happen soon, I just know it, but how could I stop it, eh, I was the one who wanted to protect Eli from all his escapades, oh he's a demon as pernicious as he is seductive, was Daniel's reply, you didn't see it coming, but most of all, he wanted to draw Stephen's attention away from the thrall Eli had him in and all the damage he'd already done, so he asked Stephen how his book was coming, and then at once Stephen was illuminated, you know, this office of Charles's has a monastic serenity, or maybe his spirit still inhabits it, almost like a hand guiding mine as I grope my way around it, he used to say men of thirty always know everything, he hated surplus old age, it hadn't occurred to him that thirty-year-old writers often lack courage and daring, they, I, can't leap into the unknown, just grope my way, along the timid borders of convention, he had no way of knowing that, on the contrary, I always feel I've got it wrong and the passing of an older writer is like a part of myself torn away, my family in fact, leaving a void, Stephen went on, when a writer of Mexican history departs, he is the one who knows that all revolutions are betrayed, outrun by blind violence while each of us seeks only harmony in an equality quite different from the next guy's, these masters who wrote about almost a century of Latin American dictatorships and their downfall with words borrowed from an epic odyssey, they cannot be replaced, and certainly not by gutless and ambitious politicians, how I envy their manly companionship, standing shoulder to shoulder, they didn't write to get rich, but out of brotherliness, I suppose, yeah, that's it, each one irreplaceable in the brotherhood, beyond dictatorships and revolutions: Carlos Fuentes, Gabriel García Márquez, and Mario Vargas Llosa, never yielding under the pressure to write commercially acceptable work to get rich, Stephen said, the way we writers in our thirties are tempted to do in our boorishness toward writers of the past, we want millions from our very first book, lining up with literary businessmen from the first, that's where we sometimes go wrong, geez, where did all these mosquitos come from, he snapped, maybe they're attracted by the chlorine in the pool, hey, you know, I saw an iguana in the garden, he was creeping towards the arbour when I was reading there, this was Daniel thinking, was Stephen forgetting he was in the tropics, even if he didn't appreciate the beauty, then Stephen noticed a shadow approach in the large garden mirror, it was Eli running as if to hide, with another man following him. Now Fleur was remembering his first encounter with Wrath near the cathedral, at first seeing nothing more than an old man, probably just some ageing intellectual checking the concert programme, his face half hidden by a felt hat as he pulled old-fashioned steel-rimmed spectacles from his worn coat and approached Fleur, who himself had abandoned the concert-hall, feeling like a fugitive too, dazzled by the May sunshine, you're here to listen to the Mass, are you, or would it be Vespers, why don't we go inside the cathedral together, Wrath had plied Fleur with questions, Gabriel Wrath's my name, like the Wrath of God, the old man said, surely mad, thought Fleur, who paid no attention, the old man clearly knew music, and they fell to discussing it, the old man telling him he was erudite, talking to the boy as though he knew all about him, an orator's monotone, and as he spoke, Fleur no longer doubted his sincerity, for his moral decline had not yet begun, what was soon to happen under the bridges, Fleur thought, reminded him of his childhood, as Wrath said, I sometimes wonder if the Devil is the incarnation of an abused child, adults cannot deny their sexual appetite for children, isn't that so, the mark on the child, the Devil's passage into that malleable little body marred forever, thus in his mistreated body, the Devil enters churches, creeping into everything, the mentor and tutor's body, oh how many of us were abused this way in rural schools, I myself grew up in the smell of incense and knowing the hideous caress of rape, for such abuses are caresses to us, our sole signs of affection, and do we even know what is happening to us, the country is as secretive as what we are subjected to, a principal or tutor brushes the nape of our neck, and we tremble from head to toe, then we bow to his supplications, such is the Devil's charisma that we can do nothing else, in this unrestrained coupling, we in turn become the Devil, he who unrestrained holds our neck in his hands, bends us toward him, thus are we in a secret plain, a jaded landscape full of silence, yes, secret and silence, our blushing bodies belaboured and broken, yes Fleur, perhaps it's true, the Devil is an abused child who's grown up with the most perverted of secrets, even the joys are secret and remain so when one is a petrified old adult, Wrath was silent after that, only to praise the music they listened to together moments later in the cathedral, some of Wrath's remarks were the result of his insanity, mad words indeed, thought Fleur, thinking himself a suspended musician, an escapee from the concert-hall where his work was played, he listened when Wrath told him resolutely, you must listen to me, you must, you see, I have chosen you for this, was it some form of sorcery, Fleur wondered, confused by the old man's nebulous eloquence, compelled to follow him, walking with him as though hypnotized, yet Fleur had the impression he'd always known this man, and nothing in him seemed frightening, and it was only when Fleur mentioned Alphonso, the utterly guiltless friend of his mother, who had sacrificed his own freedom to shelter refugees in his church, then sent to a far-away diocese as a punishment, Wrath reacted forcefully and yelled that this priest

Alphonso, like his virtuous comrades, had mounted a conspiracy to persecute Wrath and his like, yes, this same Alphonso had emphasized in writing that the names of all these predators needed to be publicized along with all the information they had managed to gather, the bishops should be under orders to send their names to the police, that was why Gabriel had changed his name to just Wrath, the justice of priest Alphonso was constantly on his trail, instead of the bishops affording him protection, now, all of a sudden, these same religious authorities and the entire hierarchy risked being blamed themselves, not only with the information obtained by Alphonso and the others but by the victims themselves coming forward, including Tai, the son he'd adopted in Asia, the threats piled up perilously along with the files, said Wrath, no, no protection anywhere, but Fleur barely heard Wrath's rushing tide of words for the the coat-collar he now raised, muffling the long, scattered and breathless monologue from beneath his hat, then remembering Fleur was beside him, Wrath turned to him, so you you used to be a street-musician, eh, well don't worry, that's just an interlude in your musical life, you'll soon be back playing concerts, fate can only be put off for so long, it always catches up with us, doesn't it, I'd like you to meet a few of my friends from the lower depths who are also musicians, my friend Su for instance, ha, he always gets his morning cigarette from me, you'd find him fascinating, the others too, all of the secret shadow-lives, deep misery does that, you know, those in hiding know it only too well, Fleur, imagine such cultivated and sophisticated men as myself condemned to twenty years in prison, no, it's unthinkable, soon not even popes and archbishops will be able to stand up for us, we'll just be accused and ineligible even for parole, the worst of pariahs, so you see I had to run, where else to hide but among other pariahs, and as for Su, well he isn't even poor, just addicted, ah but that's just another secret, you'll like him, I'll be surprized if he doesn't die of an overdose this year, pity, I really like that boy, a good musician like you, he hardly ever plays with his group any more, just in the Metro, but you won't end up that way Fleur, believe me, a long-time confessor like me knows souls, I can guess it all, criminals, priests have confessed to me without saying what they were, but I guessed the secret crimes hidden behind their slick confessions, I saw through them and knew it all, then approved of their secret shame, all the things they didn't say, like me, approving the most monstrous sin, a string of rapes, but could you really call them rapes, I wondered about that when it came to child-abuse, does it really count as much, you see, for me, evil had already ceased to exist, I was evil itself in disguise, a feeling of faintness, nothingness, especially rage and impotence, Wrath repeated, now, thought Fleur, he'd really like to meet Su, there was some honour in being a street-musician like so many all over Europe, not barefoot beggars as Fleur himself had been, playing his flute with Kim and her tambourine, those others played in cities everywhere, not shamefully spread out against a wall, too drunk to stand up, Su as Wrath described him, was closer to Fleur in his poverty, so he said he'd like to meet Su, and Wrath had said, follow me my young friend, and suddenly, as if in a flash, there was Su in silhouette, his frail shadow joined to others wandering the beaches at night, shadows belonging to Kim, Jérôme the African and his ramshackle bicycle festooned with bottles of water like sleighbells, even the shadows of the dogs, Max and Damien, all plunged in the desert of sand, even on chilly May nights, I don't understand, Wrath said, why you aren't proud to be the musician you are, you have to change that, it's a real weakness, you can't disappoint the people who've placed their faith in you, Fleur listened astonished at the man's perceptiveness, as though they'd always known one another, Wrath had unmasked his hidden side assuredly as his father and grandfather had ever done, plain folk that they were, though they had encouraged him to leave despite his mother's insistence on keeping him by her side, Fleur was sad at not having called them since the divorce, he'd loved them very much, rarely was Fleur insensitive to the advice of a male presence, such as Wrath at this moment or the composer-pianist Franz who had awarded him the prize and not minded a bit that the boy was a street musician sleeping out on the beach at night with his dog, the other jurors, though, had judged Fleur's music to be too dramatic and noisy, too full of pathos, no, this opera or *New Symphony* as he called it, was to Franz a work of inspiration, full of the incoherences of our time, yes indeed, such mastery of voice and instrument, he definitely had to be rewarded with a European concert tour, Franz, born in Kiev to musician-parents had started his own musical studies at age five, and at thirteen during their exile, he had his first concert-tours in the United States, and so as a product of exile himself, he could understand Fleur's music, that chaos of painful feelings, of fear and the inner dislocation this music elicited, all of it meant his place was on the podium according to Franz, and according to Wrath, he would return to it, you've just had a moment of panic, that's all, I'll take you to the station myself so you don't miss your train, he went on protectively and ever so slightly haughty, as Fleur trod his way hypnotized toward the hell of Wrath and of Su, suddenly so tranquil, as though someone had sealed up his eyes to prevent him seeing anything that went on around him, yes, he thought, this was how their first encounter had gone, Fleur simply had confidence in this elderly music connoisseur, that's all he was, only later did he notice the tinge of grey in the face below that hat, the colour of field-stone under the bridges piercing eyes of terrifying lucidity from beneath the wrinkled forehead, Fleur could sense the miserable conditions of Wrath and those like him, men, women, children, some seemed very young, clinging to their mothers, maybe it was just temporary for them, not real vagabonds and bums, after all they did travel together, as Wrath pointed out, it was an exodus from all parts, and he seemed to be the lord-and-master of the place, the lead man in this procession of the displaced swept along with him by the the power of decay, a river from hell it seemed, though it was really just a pretty river mirroring the sunlight of late afternoon and the trees about to flower, where birdsong could be heard with the happy chatter of people out for a walk, mixing with the wretched but not seeing them, just absorbed in the birth of spring, it was, as Wrath said, a port like any other with the noise of boats and freight transport, one has to bunk down somewhere, he said, while Fleur thought, watching him surface again from his sojourn in the earth's deepest shadows, the gloomy hell he dwelled in with those he called his own, there was music that must be written in a syncopated song like sobs, all the voices and silenced sounds he heard as a mute and hopeless pleading. While he wrote, Daniel thought of times when Augustino hid in his room, still furnished for a child with its old toys and videos, now deserted after such a long time, a poster on the wall testifying to his growth into self-consciousness, brutal perhaps, yet unknown to his parents though they all lived together, it showed a woman prostrate before the walls of a monastery in the mountains of Tibet, recalling the words of Rémi that women were the most stoic in the spectacular scenes of war and discrimination that split man from man, Daniel admired the courage of the woman defiantly praying against the humiliation of her oppression in China, though she was in danger of death at any instant, posed with her arms and face pressed into the muddy earth, and he thought of Augustino, not so long ago, coming home to visit his bed-ridden grandmother, he was fully capable of acknowledging the generosity of Mère to her beloved grandson as he sat reading to her, and she'd always called him that, sometimes touching his forehead as though reminiscing for the last time about the child she'd loved so much, do you still remember, she said to him, the names of all those flowers, the slowness of the African Lily opening its corollae, and he would nod, and go on reading, often interrupted by Franz on one of his morning visits, a child or two of his own under his arm, grandsons to whom he was already giving piano lessons, and proud to have had several wives and children so late in life, descendants are the best thing to have, he said, apart from music of course, oh and the latest opera was still not finished, delayed by an unexpected flu, ah Esther my dear, it's just a bunch of germs we need to ward off, here I am on my feet again, you need to do likewise, dear Esther, never mind that doctor of yours, I'm overworked, that's all, he sighed, if we believed their statistics, we'd all be dead, see how strong I am, even though it was a bit tiresome, but I've too much to do to be laid low by the flu, he told her with another sigh, what with teaching orchestra-leading to the girls who'll replace me, it's time women started conducting, God yes indeed, my sister the pianist made me realize that, now would I have thought of that all by myself, eh, but perhaps not with he same fervour, for so long I was preoccupied with my composition, but then I did think of women too much in another way, you see Esther, that's the way it is with manliness, just look at these lovely children I have around me, now wouldn't you say they're my greatest accomplishment of all? Ah but the women who've loved you Franz, have cried such tears because of you, Mère's look seemed to say as she leaned on his arm, had she said this out loud, perhaps, for Frantz felt a slight note of reproach creep into the air of her perfumed room, I'm so pleased, Esther dear, that Augustino's come to spend a few days with you, he said before tucking the young ones under his arms and running for the car, ah my hour has struck, and I must get back to work, besides I promised the kids I'd take them to the beach, come my angels, yes, that's how it went when he still came home to visit her, Daniel thought alone in Augustino's room. Robbie had joined Petites Cendres for his run, as he often did a few hours before the first show at seven, more like speed-walking really, relaxing now in his boy-clothes, jeans and white sneakers, his sensual nose and lush lips breathing in all they could of the sea air, still warm as it unfolded from around his body, Robbie was telling his friend about his day, how he'd met Alexandra and Leonie who'd be sharing Petites Cendres' room that night, well, you know I usually sleep out on the veranda in my hammock next to my caged birds anyway, was the reply, and the girls are looking for an apartment that will take their dogs, so I'll have company, better than nightmares, eh, besides it's not for long, they'll soon find The Acacia Gardens pretty tame, Robbie noted, so don't get too comfortable, they're going to renovate some of the apartments, and after that, they'll pick up their hammers and nails and be off to all the celebrations and anti-homophobia parades, that's what they said, boy, they're not afraid of anything, not even the herd of Bulls with their tear-gas and all, marriage is for anyone, including them, such happy newlyweds, so no fear, not even of the Bulls, for their youth and their health are their shields, they'll know how to take care of themselves, yeah, said Petites Cendres, but they're still a bit young, I wish I could hold onto them a little longer, protect them, you know, he added, specially Leonie the one with the guy's hat and the brim pushed up, a mysterious look under those long lashes, I was thinking what a sweet little sister she'd make, and with girls you can laugh, what with all their weird and wonderful ideas, if they just weren't always on the phone, we could talk some, what are they going to do in the middle of the Bull herd, Robbie, no, I don't want them to go, I mean those fanatics have weapons, and they don't, their just innocent kids with other fanatical kids in arms, they'll protest and fight, Robbie answered, that's what youth is for, later you're too tired for that stuff, I mean we're not going to face the herd, are we, just let them rain down insults and abuse on the hatemongers, then you wake up and find out some transsexual friend's been found in a ditch with a bullet through his head, and everyone acts oh-so-surprised, that's the kind of thing that happens way too often, look, Victoire phoned the Gardens for an emergency room in a few days because his life's been threatened in Mississippi, Yinn's the one who's going to introduce him to the head of volunteers and residents, she won't be the first to come here on the run, it'll be a bit like seeing Fatalité all over again, but Victoire confided in Yinn that if she came out to all her girlfriends and male friends — and there are lots of them, all straight, because she played the game for a long time — the woman cocooned in her couldn't stand the hiding and the secrets any more and burst out, if she were open and honest about wanting to be a woman, that all the people who'd admired her as a man would turn around and destroy her, she didn't say what kind of circles she moved in, but she often mentioned courageous men, friends, brothers, like some sort of army for men of valour, yeah, that's it, Robbie said, but how can we know, obviously she's still too afraid, but here she'll be safe, and she's not convalescing or even sick, she's brimming with life, her ailment is fear, secrecy, the pain of shame thrust upon her, she's like one of those nestlings under an incubator lamp that you have to feed every hour or so, Petites Cendres said, that's what Mabel told me to do with my doves and mourning-doves because they had no parent, but Victoire is no bird, she's a man emerging as a woman, a pretty big man, too, Yinn told me, but fragile as my little ones and in need of watching, the transformation isn't over yet, still a few more operations to go, step-by-step as Yinn says, all we need from people in the Acacia Gardens is that each be responsible for him — or herself, we owe it to us, fulfillment and happiness, since rent is low, we can shrug off some of the material needs and just concentrate on getting well and reconciling with life, the Gardens are transforming too, thanks to all those volunteers, but it's ours to make work above all, Robbie said, and we aren't there yet, we're out of space, but soon we'll have more, there are those who leave us though, said Petites Cendres sadly as he slowed the pace, what a gorgeous day for jogging, Robbie said pretending not to hear, you ought to work out more often, he laughed, what about that family Dr. Lorraine wants to bring from South Africa, those kids are like baby birds with no parents, just grandparents left to give them warmth and shelter, the doc's determined the kids won't be wiped out like their parents, the new meds we've got here will see to that, she may be right, replied Petites Cendres sceptically, his heart tightening with unspeakable tenderness every time Robbie deliberately dropped Yinn's name, as though it stopped him short each time, and he thought of those who'd left them or were about to, who knows where or how, as their friends or relatives collected their bits of furniture with a van in the pink shadow of evening on the palms, so quick you didn't notice, be it the stealthy departure of the emaciated ones behind the mosquito-screens to whom Brilliant brought the evening meal, not this time though, no need for it, no appetite, maybe tomorrow, knowing there'd be no one behind the screen fevered and staring into emptiness, Petites Cendres knew he could tell by the arrival of Reverend Stone sliding along the wall murmuring stubborn consolation to each of them, repeating that the Father Magnanimous had gathered another into his kingdom, where all life begins and remains, everyone could hear his prayers out by the sea, like the day Fatalité had been buried beneath the waves with orchids and roses, enough, yelled Robbie, enough praying, Reverend Stone, really, Dieudonné was there too, oh yes, that announced a departure more than anything else, his back bowed under the weight of purple flame-tree flowers, so absorbed one couldn't even see his face buried in his hands, a black swan that had brushed the white walls of houses and cottages with awkward wings, unconsolable at having once more to say farewell without having time to say he'd miss them as friends, and he'd joined Robbie in yelling, no more praying, with Robbie, let's all be quiet, silence all, and after the trucks had driven away, the echo of tennis balls from the courts where the young people were playing, and a sudden burst of energetic voices reminded all of them, Petites Cendres in his hammock as well as Dieudonné and Stone, that this is how it was, life went on at the Gardens. Who was this coming in through the back kitchen door, someone Daniel was amazed at for not having seen him in so long, Jermaine, son of Olivier and Chuan, boy he'd grown, he was a man the same age as Samuel of course, sailing in as familiar as can be, the way he'd done so many times before as a young boy, when he skateboarded in to play chess after school, my father's not doing too well, he said, he'd really like you to come and visit him, my mum's in London for an exhibition of her models, and I'm looking after him while she's away, my dear dad's not what he used to be, depression's really eating away at him, I don't understand, he's perfectly happy when Mum's there, and this has, well, you know how down he is, and it's affecting his physical health, he can barely walk, and, how can I put this, I've stopped work on my film for now and come back from L.A. to be with him, but what I'd like most of all is for you Daniel, so respected by both my parents, they're forever talking about you and your family, to talk to Olivier and convince him to let me do an interview on film so I can show people how he struggled for years, he has so little faith in himself now, but he was such an unstoppable force, Daniel embraced

Jermaine and said, I know this is hard for you, but perhaps his past battles are precisely what has drained him, worn him out, made him so unlike his true self, then Jermaine went on with his mother's glint in his eye and her life-force radiating from him as well, her taste for and pleasure, though he spoke to Daniel with gravity and respect of what he felt for his father, this past, he said, I don't want it to be forgotten, I want him to tell it with no holding back, those painful moments in his life, the Secret he kept locked inside, all the injustice he'd undergone as a young black militant, this perhaps was the source of his depression, and I want my film to give him back the justice he deserves, Olivier the militant in the days when they set the dogs on him, or he and the others were battered by the water-cannons, not like me growing up in a privileged childhood with everything possible, he never wanted me to know, you remember how he went off in a corner to write his articles in that private pavilion of his, then phone my mother several times a day just to say he loved her and could never live without her, my mother, the beautiful, desirable Chuan, a man so melancholic and sentimental, and you know how he used to cheat just a little bit and told me I could go in there sometimes while I'm writing, just a quick kiss, and when I stood in front of him, he'd say, do you love me as much as yesterday, that's how loved and spoiled I was, never thinking for a minute until one day he told me how hard it was to be a black man and a senator, sure, I remember what he said, though I only thought about playing and didn't really listen back then, I said one day I'd have a sports car, well, he didn't let me have one, almost lecturing me the way he hardly ever did, it isn't going to happen in my lifetime, son, not while I'm your father, I have to say I was obsessed with sport cars then, and he often said, no, you study hard like Samuel, because the two of us always used to play together, games and stupid stuff too, like getting fractures when we got to racing out of control, he smiled, oh I had such a nice childhood, blissfully unaware of his past or my mother losing her family in Japan during the war, nope, they didn't want me to know any of it, I was so sheltered they realized their past lives would upset me, but now I'm aware of it, and my father's testimony has to light up the future for those who don't want to forget, yes that's it, Jermaine mused, and I know that you Daniel, you can convince him to go along with me and do the interview, no holding back, but I'm not sure he will have enough confidence in me, there's a sort of bashfulness between father and son, Jerome became so enthusiastic he even talked about the soundtrack for his film with some black musicians that Olivier admired, Papa often says how they fought prejudice alongside him with their art, it's a more conciliatory and pleasing voice than street demonstrations and facing off against the police, we'd hear Donald Byrd and his amazing trumpet innovations showing exactly how the music should be, creation isn't recreation the way most people think of it, he's not there to lead people on, but to give voice to unending revolution, there'd also be Marian Anderson and her new band leader James DePriest, there aren't many black concert masters around, and this one had polio, so he runs the orchestra from an electric wheelchair, all these, Dad says, struggled alongside him, what courage and passion it took to overcome years of segregation, yes true courage, my father says, till their art was recognized and appreciated after so many years invisible and afraid, Daniel listened to Jermaine as he pictured his grandparents' house, which his mother had designed in the Cuban style, yellow and ochre on the walls, that's where he would see Olivier once more, the same Olivier who was chased by dogs through the streets of Birmingham, it wasn't the fault of these bare-fanged creatures, one of which Olivier always kept by his side as though to tame his fear of them, not their fault that the cops had abused them into ferocity and hate against demonstrators, white or black, a forced and diffused violence so debased, Olivier said, as he stroked the head of his German Shepherd or his Doberman, saying he kept them close to appease his son at first, and now he couldn't live without them, Jermaine had grown up not knowing about his father's past, simple oversight or indifference from an only child, something he blamed himself for now, saying his political awakening had been a long time coming, finally bringing them together in this house with yellow-and-ochre walls, the father always welcoming, though he was frail and had difficulty walking and held his son's arm as he impatiently awaited Chuan's return from London, this ailment, you know, doesn't leave me much time, we really shouldn't be apart so often, but I mustn't forget she's still young and I'm not, I must stop begrudging her success and my son's too, oh he'd do anything for Jermaine, the interview, the film, the soundtrack with his favourite musicians, but as he turned his face, emaciated and ravaged by illness, toward Daniel, he asked if it was any use recalling these old struggles, eh do you, because I sometimes think and think about it, and the terrible violence toward my people is a lesson that is never learned, not ever, Olivier said with a voice that Daniel felt was as much pained as worn out. Robbie saw Petites Cendres' pace slow and his demeanour darken, so he tried to distract him by talking about the Old Sophisticate, not everyone gets into The Acacia Gardens so easily, you know, the head of volunteers just refused the Old Sophisticate, he said, no compelling reason, he said, you see after forty years of marriage he wanted to leave his wife, so why, he said, can't I have an apartment too, I put up with her for forty years, so why can't I finally live without her, he begged, but they told him, you don't leave your wife after forty years, and besides wasn't he a ranch-owner with stables, so why not go back to his horses, but my friend the Old Sophisticate complained he wasn't getting a fair shake, his wife was more and more aggressive with him, though he'd given her lots of kids and money too, his farm paid, and anyway he'd never understood a thing about women, always bordering on hysteria, though he was beyond reproach, and criticizing everything, was always well dressed when he came to the Saloon once a week, the girls out on the sidewalk wore too much makeup, and he admitted he wasn't partial to the coloured boys inside, except Robbie of course, who was only a little bit dark anyway, you had to be careful in sexual encounters, yes you had to be careful, and so he was, even when once a week he sneered at those who went into the sauna where every possible sin was committed, oh he fished in those waters as well, then returned to the bar and generously treated everyone as he rolled on the floor, he knew that though Robbie had never been his, since he was always onstage with all the painted girls singing and dancing in Jason's spotlight, he nevertheless was a bit dark, but not as dark as others or curly-headed Petites Cendres, then Robbie saw him snoring away near the foot of his stool and called him a taxi, and thus his wife saw her boozy husband emerge from the woods around their house smelling of perfume from those women he held in his arms once a week, it must be, after all, who else would smell like that, and God only knows where, that was the Old Sophisticate's secret, double infidelity and an expert liar, boys or girls at the Saloon, preferably not coloured, his wife was furious of course, and it was to save himself from her volleys that he wanted refuge in the Gardens, sure, he told Robbie, I'm an abused husband, see, so you and your friends have got to take pity on a man mistreated or I'll have twenty more years of this if I can't get in, that's how it is when you're still full of the juices of life and no one wants you any more, still you'll see I know how to act, Robbie, not like those dirty old men you youngsters have hanging around, I've still got my dignity, and all I ask is a bit of fun once a week, I'm afraid if I stay shut up with her I really will end up being an old man, that's right, and I want none of it, so please beg your friend Yinn to give me a chance to stay as I am, an older man of the world with a right to a few of life's little rewards, especially for someone as insatiable as I am, after all, you and your friends have your fun don't you, and I'll be fine at the Gardens, not exactly alone, eh, I mean you're here every day to see your curly-headed friend Petites Cendres, now that one spends all his nights waiting to pick up customers at the Porte du Baiser, oh yes, it's the Gardens for me, I just know it, please Robbie, don't forget me, okay, that's all I ask, that's the trouble with old men, people forget about them, and that's exactly what makes them old, but not me, no never, the Old Sophisticate told Robbie, Petites Cendres barely listened to Robbie distractedly, for he knew the Old Sophisticate with his fancies and dislikes only too well, in fact he was fed up with them, enough of his ramblings at the bar, though he was an old man, and you had to consider that, he thought, but his mind was really elsewhere, he was preoccupied by the arrival of Victoire, exactly who was she or he, finally emerging from a cloud of mystery and anonymity, as grand today as Fatalité was yesterday, just a foggy photo sent to Yinn's phone, but how much more well-behaved she looked with a vague smile as though trying to overcome her own bashfulness with a new image, who knows what her masculine name was before, or her life, what did it conceal, what did she do for a living, all of it hidden, all to be guessed at, thought Petites Cendres, sailor, boxer, soldier, pilot, engineer, maybe even a well-known sports figure, but in the picture she was standing wearing an oh-so-proper dress with bare, sturdy arms, tall next to her guard dog, which was pretty tall too, and watchful, it was calming to think of her, she was a woman of the future, as Léonie told Alexandra, girls with pretty dirty mouths, he thought, and they had boundless confidence in a future where labels and derogatory or accusatory words had no place, being things of a religious and divisive past, that would come about in their lifetime, though not his, words and lifestyles would no longer be the same in thirty years or more, the oddball and revolutionary idea the girls had was that we'd be living under the Reign of Poetry, where the times, like the language, would be entirely new, and all destructive, defeatist, racist or sexist labels, in fact every kind of stupidity or separation, would be eradicated, and all would be united in poetic neutrality without words of hate, as though love were repeated ad infinitum, so Alexandra said, it was truly stupendous to hear them proclaim the Reign of Poetry they so believed in, still they were so very charming in their vests that one could almost believe it all, thought Petites Cendres, and under that same reign their would be many more women astronauts like Sally Ride, the novice space traveller, so said Leonie from under the upturned brim of her boy's hat, with all the courage and ability that would long be remembered as her message of equality, and the eloquence with which she praised her long-time partner, Tam, so that many would roam space thinking of her, yet not able to marry as two women under the Reign of Closetdom, not yet able to call her spouse and still remain an astronaut, condemned by a word, but the time for such secrecy was on the wane, Leonie said, of that she was certain, but these idealistic and brainy girls surely oughta know the planet was past saving, thought Petites Cendres, everywhere deep in pockets and folds it still held madmen and madwomen brandishing their slogans of hate, and these normal-seeming maniacs, often ever-so-respectable people, looked for no better than to tear the flesh of others, he reflected, no, there would be no Reign of Poetry, people's habits don't change, Alexandra and Léonie were wrong, it was either too soon or too late, and someone had to tell them without scaring them too badly or letting them down too hard. So, said Adrien to the waiter who'd brought him his cocktail as he sat writing to his son from his deckchair, I'd like the table to be set on the platform out by the wharf right next to the ocean, and let's hope the wind doesn't get any stronger, oh by the way, my friend, what country are you from, Jamaica, Mr. Adrien, I told you earlier, I'm doing an internship here at the Grand Hotel, ah, beautiful country Jamaica, Adrien said, happy to have his table where he wanted it, will that be for dinner, the waiter asked, yes, I'm expecting a lady at any moment, I'll add more hibiscus to the vases, the ones on the table are a bit wilted from the heat, the waiter replied, and what's your name, asked Adrien notebook in hand, I mentioned yesterday my name was Simon, Mr. Adrien, ah a lovely country Jamaica, repeated Adrien, Simon, yes of course, Simon, and you're interning till autumn, you see, I do remember, Simon, yes Simon, of course I do, tomorrow I'll put a parasol by your chair so you can write, said Simon, it's school vacation and we have lots of kids, I hope they won't be bothering you too much, we can't stop them running along the beach, nor shouting, can we, oh such yelling, kids do so get under my skin, said Adrien as he rubbed his ear and cast a complicit glance at Simon, even small ones, I could never stand being near them, how is it we're forced to endure their yelling, why did the Good Lord scatter these screaming brats all over the place to torment us, and why on earth do people make so many of them, in a world as topsy-turvy as this, Simon, I understand nothing of God and his ways, do you, it does seem inscrutable, replied Simon, have you had sufficient quiet to write today, Mr. Adrien, I've done my best to keep them away from you, same as every day, but it's rare to have this many children at the Grand Hotel, couples usually travel alone, of course, I'm grateful to you, Simon, said Adrien, touched by the lad's foresight and attention, thanks to your care, I have indeed been able to write peaceably for several hours, no, the problem is that I'm still stuck on the one poem, I must have tried a hundred times, but I just can't seem to break out of it, and I don't like the title "Giving Account", but I can't seem to find another, perhaps my imagination's drying up, at that, Simon said nothing but hurried off in search of fresh hibiscus for the vases on table two and Adrien's, he'd also bring some lamp oil and ignite the tall bamboo torches along the beach as evening crept in across the shimmering sea. Well, the fever's gone down, said Dr. Dieudonné on his visit to Angel, that's a nice surprise, these sea outings are doing you good, it seems, son, but you must never forget your meds, I know your mama's careful to make sure you get them down every day, now I've got another surprise for you, there will soon be some other children here, Dr. Lorraine's bringing them from South Africa, so you'll finally have someone your own age, now what do you say, and their grandmas are coming with them, so you won't be bored, I can't wait to see the bunch of you running up and down the stairs, you haven't done much running, but with them you will, they're still healthy though, replied Angel, and so are you said the doctor, you're well on the way back, and they're just here for preventive treatment because of their parents, they've been at risk for years, he added, the thought of running in the stairwells with new kids reminded Angel of all the moves he'd made over the years with his mother whenever they were chased out of each apartment or house or whatever refuge they sought in hotels and motels with "vacancy" signs lit up, refugees right here at home, exiled and contaminated, thought Angel, there must be thousands like them all over the globe unwanted by anyone, meandering secretly, travelling by night, here in a suburban hotel, there under the blinking sign of a rural motel, Lena and Angel or others like them, sleeping in one place tonight and another tomorrow, the poorer ones even setting up camp and driving away without paying when no one was watching, Angel could remember so many different playmates he'd had fun with, but who were so hard up they wore the same unwashed clothes for a month, fleeing in shame at being homeless, fishing in hotel dumpsters when their mothers weren't looking, a discarded toy here, a piece of bread there, on the way to becoming hoods, Angel thought, but he still liked to play with them, and from the hotel window, he'd seen them running up and down the stairs and all over, shouting their rebellion in all kinds of foul language, that was their fun before inevitably moving on, angrily bouncing balls off walls, he'd've liked to play with them, but they weren't even aware he existed, contaminated by the curse in his blood, no, he envied their vitality and even their anger, stair-running and indifferent to him, and he watched them all from his window, then their mothers would call: quick, we have to leave, pushed aside again, we're not welcome here, never mind, we'll find another motel, cheaper, whatever, come on now, pity I didn't have time to wash the younger ones, okay let's go, you know the drill, follow close behind me to the car, how many times do I have to tell you, don't fish those dirty toys out of the garbage, forget them; so they ran crestfallen for the car, dishevelled and enraged, wondering why their childhoods weren't like the others', when do we get to go back to school, they'd ask, when we find somewhere they'll put up with us, their mothers would answer, I really want you to go back to school, but before that we'll stop at the first refuge we find, so you can get something to eat, then Papa will come join us, he's still got work or I don't know what would happen to us, really I don't, then the car would be gone, this was the time of evening when Angel's fever ran highest and he started coughing, oh he'd seen lots of these refugee kids in the stairwells, this was during their season of migration before he and his mother Lena were accepted, almost without a word, into the Acacia Gardens, and all the time he was under Dr. Dieudonné's care, Angel dreamed of nothing but the coming walk along the seashore, any time now, and the sunset in a blazing sky over the ocean, that's what Brilliant had promised him, and off they'd sail on pirate Captain Joe's white-masted sailboat, he had a very lucrative business in the Bahamas, no champagne, but Brilliant would supply that from a cooler, he told Lucia they'd coast along with the dolphins under the stars, sure, all of us, Lena, Misha, Lucia, and Brilliant, Lucia warned him not to drink the champagne before they left, because even now he seemed a little tipsy, but it was just the heat, he said, 'sides a little champers never hurt anyone, with Night Out balanced on her shoulder, she happily waited for them to cast off, and with Misha and Brilliant around, her sisters would probably stop following her, she had to keep putting them out of her mind, otherwise they'd never leave her in peace and she'd always be on the run from them, though Brilliant always said, calm down, Lucia dear, I guarantee they'll leave you alone, yes, she'd reply, but they have the law on their side, and what's going to happen if they prove I can't always remember things, you've got Dieudonné and me to watch out for you, he said, I'm so afraid that I keep a list of absolutely everything, just like the doctor told me, so I never draw a blank or get a date and time wrong or even forget my name, but I'll always remember my parakeet's name, Night Out, and Mabel gave her to me, oh such a wonder my bird is, my winged treasure, what does it matter if I forget my first name's Lucia, but hers is Night Out, you've heard how beautifully she sings, haven't you, Brilliant, so very prettily, she said hoping she hadn't remembered wrong, now there, calm yourself, said Brilliant, there's nothing to be afraid of any more,

Angel had an abscess in his mouth, and Dr. Dieudonné was feeling the boy's forehead and reassuring him that he had a toothache, nothing more, he'd get over it like the headaches, his recovery would be slow but sure, yes, of course it would, meanwhile Angel was anticipating the arrival of Brilliant and Misha, and his mother draped a jean jacket over him, for it was going to be chilly this evening, then he said, I'm all set Mama, and soon we'll be on the ocean, Brilliant gets so many things going, that's why he's always late. Adrien got up to wait for Charly, was it a mirage or had he really seen her strolling past the flowers and bougainvillias in the Grand Hotel gardens, she must be taking her time getting to him as she ambled along the path through the fountains while children still bathed in the glittering green water of the pools, oh what shouts, of course Simon had mentioned the school vacations that never seemed to end, how slowly she walked, sleepily, perhaps it was the heat, Adrien thought, maybe after all just a mirage of her in tight black pants and a transparent white blouse that clung to her flat breasts, she had high-heeled sandals, was it really her or someone else, he wondered, then a shadow of concern spread over his face partly masked by the slanted rays of sunlight and his hat, she sometimes hung out with a group of young women, Isaac was often surrounded by women he never tried to conquer, he was that absorbed and carried away by his creative projects, still he couldn't live without the company of women, thought Adrien, he was never without women around him, and rumour had it that Charly was one of them, in his boat, on his island, The Island No One Owns, the wildest of all his creations, paradise to the Florida Panther, even building a tower to observe the ocean, though no one else was allowed to climb the steps, and there at the majestic summit, he contemplated a world eternal, he and he alone, beige shorts and cane, the ocean at his feet, endless sky overhead, and face-to-face with the immense beauty of emptiness in all its splendid colours, nothing else but flights of eagles and their young, how had Charly managed to wheedle and manoeuvre her way into this landscape so quickly, and what on earth could she be doing there, Adrien asked himself, the iconic and titanic architect Isaac was a man of phenomenal fortune, so was Charly again up to the things she'd done to Caroline, this time, however, the risk from the greed that lodged in her heart would be incalculable, Isaac being, despite appearances, a very powerful man, and what exactly would they wreak on one another, something ignominious, he thought, Isaac was largely unaware of the fallout from his power and authority, but he was still an old man and she a young woman, so what was she doing prowling around on his territory, she to whom Adrien had nothing to offer but reciting poems to her in the limo, and what had she to offer, languid in her black slacks, to a man who would be leaving his house, Suzanne's, to their children, along with the royalties from his books, yes, there were a lot of books, but lately the critics had snubbed the theoretical strain in his poems and called him hermetic, that's all he needed at the end of his days, nothing else to keep him going, though he wasn't unduly worried, he still had his teacher's pension, but it was humiliating, no doubt about it, he had so little to offer Charly, when his good friend Isaac was master of the universe and didn't even know it, one casual glance from the top of his tower or even the bottom, would make him the master of Charly or any other woman, there were so many, and he was barely aware of his regiment of beauties, ridiculous really, he thought, Adrien felt like a jilted lover, though still glad Charly had accepted his invitation to dinner at the Grand, good old Simon had reserved his special table, number two by the ocean, and while what was surely a mirage in a chauffeur's cap approached him, Adrien thought tonight would be the night he finished his poem, "Giving Account" had him in its grip for long enough, yet there were still some lines to add, the challenge in this poem being that he really did have to give an accounting for his old and withered soul, even this encounter, here and now, had to be written, unless of course Charly decided not to show, and this turned out to be just a mirage, old Faust meeting his devil, if the devil could ever be this attractive, he mused, in that case, the poem would have to be fleshed out, and so he went on daydreaming in the evening breeze with eyes staring far off. Here was Mai's face again on the bluish screen, don't forget to get everyone together for my graduation, Papa, she told him, he'd stopped work to talk to the flickering image on the screen, yes, he said, I'll get the whole family together, Daniel told her, and Mama will be back soon, a lot of people have been hurt in the demonstrations in Moscow, I know Mama's there with them, young women writers have been thrown in jail for their books and still haven't been released, Daniel told Mai that Mélanie was fine and wondered if this meant a return to the Stalinist period, she really is quite worried about the censored writers, oppression always starts with poets and writing, Mélanie said, I'll get all of you together except maybe Augustino, yes, said Daniel, Augustino whose voice has become so sad now, but tell me, Mai, are your studies going well, not going out too much to celebrate with your friends, right? Well, Papa, you know I don't just study day and night, she told him, he was struck by the recollection that she so loved going out with friends, but not as much as before, studying in the silence of the university library or in the noisy dorms or stretched out on her bed awash in the usual disorder, though no trace of the cats, dogs, and birds she was used to at home, studying for exams, oh so seriously, cheek on fist and hair in her face, meanwhile a young man suffering from paranoia—his country's government truly was plotting against him, as were teachers and fellow students— had been expelled for violent behaviour, only violent words in reality, to the effect that he would kill them all, while Mai studied for her finals, he burned sacrifices before a potted human skeleton in his parents' yard, an entire ritual screened from their view by a tent, they never noticed anything he did, thinking he was just a child like any other, a bit difficult maybe, but once he'd played the saxophone well in school, now he was turned away wherever he went, they had no idea, and while Mai studied, this odd young man, his parents, oblivious to what he was doing in their basement, was stockpiling munitions, guns and revolvers, one of them an expensive Glock he'd bought from a merchant who never asked for his ID, it held thirty rounds, almost like holding a machine-gun, thought the boy, it was intoxicating, what you got there, said the seller, is a real powerful weapon, the best, the young man must have been prey to some psychosis or other, his words disjointed and punctuated with cries and laughter as though from the effect of drugs, his skin reddened in places as though in the grip of some hidden dementia, trembling hands and irrational language tinged with violence from the outset, sinister forewarnings and strangled threats, yet the shop-owner noticed none of this, being too busy with other clients, so great was the demand and getting greater all the time, and this is how the young man had managed to accumulate so much ordinance in his basement, all set for the Great Attack to take place with his Glock in hand when every student was gathered at Mai's graduation, and Daniel would need only to turn on his computer to see the extent of the massacre and hear Mai herself crying out, Papa, don't come anywhere near the campus, Mama and Papa, don't come any closer, we heard an explosion, and there are police cars, now Daniel would see graduates fleeing along with their professors, gowns and flying mortarboards amid the smoke, then thirty shots from the avenging Glock whistled through the air, killing, killing till each student fell flat on the ground, Mai lay on the grass with them, some with bloody perforations to the head, but for the time being, Mai was still here against the blue background of the screen, Papa, you know all I've done is study the past months, you know, but I wanted to tell you, I'm afraid for Mama in Moscow, and I was afraid when she was in China too, someone fired blindly into a crowd of demonstrators, lots of people dead, she'll be back on Sunday, Daniel said soothingly, don't worry sweetheart, concentrate on your studies, and now the Great Attack is over, and the police have caught the young man who with seeming arrogance says, I've done well what I set out to do, look at my fine massacre will you, just the way I planned it, no one in my sights survives, not even the little nine-year-old who just wandered onto the campus to play an hour before graduation, not even her, no, not a one, I got them all, now Mai reappeared on the darkening screen, this time against a background of trees and forests and wearing her white sweater, her pierced ears visible, though the image jumped around too much, and she was telling her father that she was ready for the big day, and everything would be just fine, laughing, she said, Papa, you know how much I love you, don't you? There's no point in waiting for them, Wrath said, definitely not, they will make a triumphal entry into cities and nations, you can't imagine how these millions of kids will invade and pillage us as they flood out of the ghettoes and internment camps they've been shoved into and piled up in, their parents too, in Bulgaria and wherever else, hiding behind discriminatory strictures, yes, you good citizens of Bulgaria, head back to your nice clean homes, and you others, Bohemians, on the other side of the street, away to your slums, no sewers, no clean water, back to whatever shops are left open for you to starve in, go on, get out, yes, they'll be here in their millions, with their kids on horseback and their brothers and sisters and parents riding in the carts behind them, to lay waste when the day of revolution comes, undesirables no younger than twelve, upright on horseback and howling with rage, the young bear-tamer expelled from Romania will be there too, and so they will destroy a world that has left them out and trod them down, oh to see the day these outraged children will triumph, said Wrath in his stentorian voice and placing his hand lightly on Fleur's shoulder, as though already resigned to the boy's departure with Su, you want to go before I've even finished my confession, don't you, look why don't you take him as far as the Metro, he's so fragile my Rising Sun, oh I know that dawn will bring him back to me for his morning cigarette, yes I know all, and you Fleur, though you may not know it yet, or perhaps you'd rather pretend, you are on the way to your own kind of concert-hall triumph, I've told you, haven't I, that none of us escapes his fate, but for now Fleur could only think about Kim and her dog Damien on the beach at night with Max and Jérôme the African falling in with the procession Wrath had just foretold at the borders of countries and the gates of cities, as though on the point of bursting forth into darkening nightfall, crossing bridges, the twelve-year gypsy horseman, the bear-tamer, seemingly aflame, as though surrounded by a circle of fire, shot at as they advanced like martyr cavaliers, disposable kids thrown away, like Kim herself or Jérôme the African, and those enemies of mine who think we don't love children, he shouted, our persecutors leagued against us, yes, that Alphonso for instance, your mother's friend, he and his kind who think us enemies of childhood, oh but us, we priests of evil, what have we to love if not childhood, beaten, starved and brutalized like us, many with no one but other orphans to love, to cuddle and torment, no right even to explain, just hand us over to Justice, sure violated as boarders ourselves by teachers, tutors and those same religious orders that persecute us now, the venomous breath of that Old Woman tonight, you, Wrath, yes you, I'll see you before a judge, let me tell you though you know already, you killed Tai, your adopted son you called him, before he could turn you in, yes, oh yes, listen to me Wrath, the judge, the court, now don't you listen to her Fleur, don't believe a word she says, her brain's scrambled, said Wrath, and the rotund man seemed to be speaking kindly now, you mustn't let down those who've placed their trust in you, you're a musician, and as for Tai, well, I speak about him when next we meet, for I know we will, really I do, Fleur listened and saw his sudden benevolence was not without a cruelty of its own, come, come, we must be off, he said ushering Fleur and Su toward the stone steps, Su at once to his friends in the Metro, for midnight would be too late, no one left to hear them play, no one to panhandle from, too late for the outstretched hand, and you Fleur, remember my words to you now, had I killed Tai, as this Old Witch says, well, once upon a time my superiors would have protected me, of course they would, then sent me and my Secret to some abbey in France, yes, once, or maybe to a monastery in Mexico where none would know of my crimes, total impunity, there are many others living out their lives the same way, and if Tai hadn't betrayed me, I would have ended up that way too, but he made me a pariah, of course he was fully justified, but fear not, I spared him for so long because I loved him too much, oh yes, I did, but an accident one day, an unforeseeable tragedy, yes, I did spare him for so long, Wrath repeated, well what more can I say, it's time to go, do it now or I'll take you back to the hotel myself, just by the marina not far from here, you know they're all sheltered, those who lie and hide, guilty of crimes small and great, yes, they are all protected you know, the Statute of Secrets keeps them safe, oh yes, the mother of all secrets keeps her peace, no, you see, I won't be going to prison as Tai would have wished, they always run interference for me and my Secret, these words, these rasping words of Wrath would still be sounding in his ears the next day on the train to Geneva and for the rest of his concert-tour, so would Su's words right before he disappeared into the Metro with his sheet music under his arm, Su who'd told Fleur, don't believe him, he's not as he says, Gabriel Wrath has saved me more than once, see that bench over there, more than once I stopped breathing from an overdose, and he saved me, and he'll do it again, I think, so said Su in his broken accent, Su so skinny he was no more than a shadow coughing in the night, Fleur answered under his breath, uh-hunh, he'll save you so he can exploit you some more, to the last drop of you, nothing left, sure, Wrath will do that, he thought of her, Clara, as he listened to a Mendelson quartet through his earbuds on the train, she played the violin with such virtuosity, in her he had lost something he'd never find again, what was it, the string quartet made him think it was her playing, and through the magnificence of the music filtered the insidious words of Wrath, he who denied killing Tai, and perhaps he hadn't, Wrath living in the hell of the Secret like the others, the invisible world of pariahs, reading the concert programme in front of the cathedral, Gabriel Wrath, an old connoisseur of music, a noble panhandler he had not recognized but had followed down there, so far off, along the River of Hell where he said he'd never again see the light of day, and now the music on the train and thoughts of Clara, yes, back to the light of day, he thought. It's time now, almost seven o'clock, I've got to get back to the cabaret, Robbie said to Petites Cendres, who suddenly found himself running along the seashore alone, Robbie was off to get ready for the show wearing Yinn's dress and jewellery, summer was coming and there would be new costumes for the girls to wear, revealing and spectacular, flowery, Robbie said, sure, plenty of flowers, Petites Cendres was drenched in sweat but glad he'd run this much, now slowly loping toward The Acacia Gardens, his own gardens, the lights gradually starting to come out as the sea quenched the sun's purple rays, though it was still practically daylight, then he saw a car with tinted windows, so dark in fact that he couldn't see the driver, and out stepped a shockingly thin man with a suitcase in his hand and clothes as dark as his skin, then Dieudonné went toward him and bid him welcome to the Gardens, both heading for the hospital via the Green Palm Walk, and Petites Cendres remembered what Dieudonné had said to Dr. Lorraine, there was slavery, there was segregation, but the same poverty and racism still needed battling in the corridors of shame and secrecy of the South, almost as many victims as in the Sahara or the rest of Africa, oh yes, almost, and the young man dropped off by the anonymous limo might be one of the victims of ignorance and homophobia, Petites Cendres might see him again, was there still hope for him or was it too late, slowly he made his way to the stairs that led to Lena and Angel's veranda, he heard Angel laugh as he came down the steps with Misha and told Petites Cendres to come along with them, we're going out on the ocean with Brilliant's friend Captain Joe, and Petites Cendres said, sure he'd go, and Brilliant hippity-hopped his way after them trying to catch Misha who was chasing doves and turtledoves in the garden, don't bark so loud, he said, we're going out in a boat, hey don't bark like that, but Angel rewarded him with happy laughter.

About the Author

Photo by Jill Glessing

MARIE-CLAIRE BLAIS is the internationally revered author of more than twenty-five books, many of which have been published around the world. In addition to the Governor General's Literary Award for Fiction, which she has won four times, Blais has been awarded the Gilles-Corbeil Prize, the Medicis Prize, the Molson Prize, and Guggenheim Fellowships. She divides her time between Quebec and Florida.

About the Translator

NIGEL SPENCER has won the Governor General's Literary Award for Translation with three novels by Marie-Claire Blais: *Thunder and Light*, *Augustino and the Choir of Destruction*, and *Mai at the Predators' Ball*, which was also a finalist for the QWF Cole Foundation Prize for Translation. He has translated numerous other works and films by and about Marie-Claire Blais, Poet Laureate Pauline Michel, Evelyn de la Chenelière, and others. He is also a film-subtitler, editor, and actor now living in Montreal.